## "It's Mr. Cowboy," Beth yelled, racing to the door.

Then to Sophie's utter dismay, her daughter said to Tanner, "Houston, we have a problem."

Tall, lanky and lean, with wide denim-clad shoulders that looked perfect for leaning on, Tanner Johns was every woman's fantasy cowboy.

Not *her* fantasy cowboy, of course, but—

"What's the problem, er, Houston?" His gaze rested on Sophie.

Sophie couldn't explain because there was something wrong with her breathing. As in, she couldn't. Then Davy came racing down the stairs, tripped on the perpetually loose runner at the bottom tread and tumbled headlong into the cowboy's arms. Tanner caught her son and held on just long enough to make sure Davy could stand on his own.

"Something I said?" he joked, winking at her.

The man *winked* at her! The control Sophie had almost recovered vanished. She figured she probably looked like a beached fish, gulping for air. Stupidly, she wished she'd had time to fix her hair.

*Where's your independence now?*

**Lois Richer** loves traveling, swimming and quilting, but mostly she loves writing stories that show God's boundless love for His precious children. As she says, "His love never changes or gives up. It's always waiting for me. My stories feature imperfect characters learning that love doesn't mean attaining perfection. Love is about keeping on keeping on." You can contact Lois via email, loisricher@yahoo.com, or on Facebook (loisricherauthor).

## Books by Lois Richer

### Love Inspired

#### Wranglers Ranch

*The Rancher's Family Wish*

#### Family Ties

*A Dad for Her Twins*
*Rancher Daddy*
*Gift-Wrapped Family*
*Accidental Dad*

#### Northern Lights

*North Country Hero*
*North Country Family*
*North Country Mom*
*North Country Dad*

#### Healing Hearts

*A Doctor's Vow*
*Yuletide Proposal*
*Perfectly Matched*

Visit the Author Profile page at Harlequin.com for more titles.

# The Rancher's Family Wish

## Lois Richer

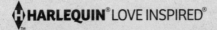

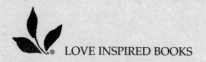

LOVE INSPIRED BOOKS

Recycling programs for this product may not exist in your area.

ISBN-13: 978-0-373-81919-5

The Rancher's Family Wish

Copyright © 2016 by Lois M. Richer

www.Harlequin.com

**Printed in U.S.A.**

Fan into flame the gift of God that is within you.
—*2 Timothy* 1:6

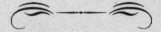

For James,
who teaches me about love and trust.

# Chapter One

"Mr. Cowboy!"

Lost in thoughts of his upcoming meeting, Tanner Johns barely registered the call of the child standing outside the door of the Tucson grocery store he'd just left.

"Hey, Mr. Cowboy!"

When the call came a third time, Tanner realized the girl had to be addressing him since there was no one else in the parking lot wearing cowboy boots and a Stetson, no one else who could even remotely be called a cowboy. He walked toward the child, taken aback by her extraordinary beauty. The piercing scrutiny of intense blue eyes enhanced her ivory skin and flaxen hair. He was a few feet away when he noticed the obvious signs of Down syndrome.

"Were you calling me?" Tanner glanced around to be certain.

"Uh-huh." Her smile made her skin glow.

"Why?" Tanner automatically smiled back. This little cutie was a looker with a grin that would melt the most weather-beaten hide.

"'Cause you're a cowboy and cowboys have ranches." Her bell-like voice carried on January's breeze as it whispered across blacktop shimmering in the Arizona heat.

Several people turned to study them. After a glimpse at Tanner their focus veered to the child, benevolent smiles widening when they spied the big cage at her feet. Wait a minute—rabbits? How had he missed that?

"A ranch is a good place to keep bunnies," she said.

"Uh, how many are there?" Tanner couldn't decipher one ball of fur from another.

"Only eight." She was probably five or six, he guessed. Sadness filled her voice as she explained, "We can't keep them anymore."

"I see." In spite of Tanner's reluctance to get involved, her innocence evoked a memory long buried inside him. Had he ever been that guileless?

"What happened to your face, Mr. Cowboy?" The question was open and honest. Tanner liked her steady stare better than others' quick gawks. Empathy beamed out from her blue eyes. "Does it hurt?"

"A little," he admitted. "I scratched myself on a wire fence."

"People stare at you." She nodded. "They stare at me, too. It's 'cause we're different."

"They stare at you because you're beautiful." Affection for this spunky child flared inside him. "And because you're special." He meant her Down syndrome.

"I'm not special." She shook her blond head firmly. "I'm just me. Mama says I'm exactly the way God made me." The happiness wreathing her round face made Tanner wish he'd had a mother like hers. His brain skittered away from that sensitive subject.

"Where is your mom?" Tanner glanced around curiously.

"Getting my brother." She pointed to a young woman with glossy, shoulder-length hair. It was clear the mom was trying to reason with a reluctant boy whom she held by one arm as she drew him forward. Her brightly flowered sundress billowed around her slim figure. She looked too young to have a daughter and a son. "That's Davy. He gets mad. A lot."

"What's your name?" Tanner forced his gaze from the brunette's lovely face to the girl in front of him. Mother and daughter shared translucent skin that seemed to bloom from within, but that's where the resemblance between the cute mom and this blonde sweetheart ended.

"I'm Beth. I'm almost six." When she grinned, dimples appeared in her apple cheeks.

"Pleased to meet you, Beth." Tanner held out a hand. He suppressed a laugh when she shook it heartily, her face completely serious. Beth's trusting gaze made him feel ten feet tall.

"Cowboys have horses, don't they?" Beth scanned the parking lot with a frown.

"Yes." Tanner choked down his mirth. "But today I left Samson at the ranch."

Beth's mother arrived breathless, studying him with a protective look flickering in her cocoa-toned eyes. Beauty certainly ran in this family.

"Hello. I'm Tanner Johns. Beth was just asking if I'd take her rabbits to my ranch."

"Will you?" A desperation the harried mother couldn't mask leached through her words before she huffed a laugh. "Sorry, that was rude. I'm Sophie Armstrong. This is my son, Davy—David."

"Nice to meet you both." Tanner took one look at the surly-faced boy and returned his attention to the easy-on-the-eyes mother.

"So can you take the rabbits?" The pleading in Sophie's voice was hard enough to resist, but that sound—half hope, half desperation—that's what got to Tanner. "I'd be very grateful."

"I—uh—" *You should have walked away, Tanner.*

"Do we have to give them all away, Mama?" Beth's gaze implored her mother to rethink her decision.

"I'm sorry but we do, honey. Mrs. Jones is very upset that the bunnies got out of their pen again and ate her flowers." The gentleness of Sophie's "mom" voice and the tender brush of her fingers against her daughter's flaxen head didn't need translation. She loved this child.

"Who cares about stupid old rabbits?" Davy scoffed. "Good riddance."

The words were a bluff to hide his anger. Tanner knew that because as a kid he'd used that same tone when life had jabbed him with reality once too often. But when Beth's blue eyes watered and her bottom lip wobbled, Tanner's chest tightened.

"Davy, that's mean," his mother reproved. "Beth loves the rabbits."

"She shouldn't. We always have to let go of stuff we love." The boy turned away to scuff his toe against a hump in the pavement, head bent, shoulders stiff.

Sophie's face fell and her amazing smile dimmed. Though Tanner understood the pain behind the words, he wanted to ream out the kid for hurting his lovely mother and sister.

*Whoa! You don't do getting involved, Tanner,*

his brain scoffed. *Never have, though Burt tried his best to teach you. Walk away.*

But two pairs of eyes, one a rich Arizona sky blue and one dark as the dust trails on Mount Lemmon's highest slopes, wouldn't let him leave.

"I can't—that is, uh, I don't know anything about keeping rabbits." Tanner gazed longingly at his truck, his way of escape. Why had he answered Beth's call in the first place?

"Okay, thanks anyway." Sophie smiled politely as her fingers squeezed Beth's shoulder. "Come on, kids. Let's get these guys loaded up. We'll have to take them to the pet shelter. I don't dare take them home again or Mrs. Jones will call the landlord."

"Old bag," Davy muttered almost under his breath.

"Manners, David," his mother reproved. "Now let's get moving. I'm working tonight, remember?"

"Again," Davy complained in a grumpy tone.

"Yes, again. Because that's how I pay for those new sneakers you're wearing. So carry the cage, Davy, and let's go." Sophie Armstrong offered Tanner a distracted smile before urging the children forward.

As they walked away Tanner heard Beth protest.

"This morning you said the pet shelter can't

keep them," she said. "What will happen to our bunnies, Mama?"

"God will take care of them." Sophie paused long enough to glance Tanner's way. He thought he glimpsed a hint of guilt in her brown eyes before she resumed her speed-walk to a red van. "After all, He cares for the sparrows and the lilies of the field, remember?"

Nice sentiment but her tone held no assurance.

*It's not your problem.* That did nothing to lift the blanket of guilt weighing down Tanner's shoulders. As he turned from watching Davy wrangle the cage into the van, his gaze slid past then returned to the logo printed on the side.

Sophie's Kitchen—Home-Cooked Food Without the Hassle.

*Home-cooked.* Tanner studied the bag in his hand.

*Doughnuts again?* In his head he heard the other church ushers' laughter. *Is that all you ever eat, Tanner?*

An idea sprang to life. He whirled around and saw Sophie, er, Mrs. Armstrong getting into her van. "Wait."

She frowned at him but waited for his approach. "Is something wrong?"

"No, yes—" He pointed at the writing on her vehicle. "You make food? For people to eat?"

"That's usually what they do with it." Amusement laced her voice.

"Do you ever make desserts? Or treats for coffee time?" Tanner felt ridiculous. But the thought of serving the same old store-bought doughnuts he always provided, the thought of overhearing the same snarky comments made him wait, albeit impatiently, for her response.

"Cakes, tarts, that kind of thing? Sure." She noticed Beth licking her lips and winked. Eyes dancing, Sophie looked young and carefree, not at all motherly.

What would it be like to be loved by a mom like her?

She frowned. "Look, I'm in a hurry—"

Tanner took a leap of faith. "I'll take the rabbits and make a home for them on the ranch in exchange for something."

"What?" Suspicion darkened her brown eyes.

"You making me some kind of dessert for tonight." Sophie's face said she wasn't sold on the trade. Hoping to sweeten the deal, Tanner glanced at Beth. "You could bring your kids to see the rabbits in their new home if you want, to make sure they're okay."

Sophie's eyebrows drew together. "What kind of dessert?"

"I don't care." He glanced down at the bag he still clutched. "As long as it's not doughnuts." He knew from the furrow on her forehead that she was considering his offer.

"You haven't given me much notice," she complained.

"Can't help it. That's the deal." Tanner tipped back on the heels of his boots, Stetson in hand, and waited while she deliberated. "There will be twelve of us."

"All men?" Sophie asked.

"Yes. Does that matter?" She nodded. "Why?" he asked curiously.

"Well, for one thing, women often appreciate different desserts from men, say something like cheesecake over pie," Sophie explained.

"Pie?" Tanner's stomach tap-danced in anticipation. "You could make pies for twelve people for tonight?"

"You'd only need three, maybe four." She tapped her chin. "That's not the problem."

"What is?" Could she see he was almost salivating at the mere thought of cinnamon-scented apple pie with a scoop of vanilla ice cream dripping down its sides?

"I have a catering job tonight, which means I couldn't possibly bake *and* deliver your pies today." When she shook her head, strands of shiny chocolate-toned hair flew through the air in an arc then fell back perfectly into place.

Tanner loved chocolate. Even more so now.

"I'm sorry, I can't do it."

"But you don't even know where I live." He wasn't giving up so easily.

"Doesn't matter. I don't have time to bake and deliver," she said. "If it could be tomorrow—?"

"It has to be today. Maybe I could pick them up. Where do you live?" He noted her hesitation. Why not? She had a couple of kids to think of. "Or perhaps your husband could meet me somewhere with them?"

"I'm a widow." The note of defiance buried in her comment intrigued Tanner.

"Well, I could pick them up," he offered. She wrinkled her nose. "Would it make a difference to you if my pastor vouched for me?" Even as Tanner said it, he wondered what his life had come to that he was willing to ask someone to vouch for him in order to get pie.

"I don't know." She hesitated.

"The meeting tonight is for our church ushers' group. I'm head usher so it's at my place and I'm supplying the food," he explained before she could say no. "We get together every three months or so to organize the schedule of who's covering which services when at Tanque Verde First Community Church."

"Hey, that's where we go," Davy said from the backseat.

"I thought you seemed familiar." The furrow

of worry disappeared from Sophie's forehead. "You're Burt Green's successor at Wranglers Ranch."

She knew Burt? Well, of course she did. Tanner figured pretty well everyone at First Community Church must know about the burly rancher and the transient kids he'd often brought to church.

"I was sorry to hear of Burt's passing." Sophie glanced at the van's clock, hesitated a moment then nodded. "Okay. It's a deal. You can pick up your dessert at my place in exchange for taking the rabbits. But I'm not promising pie."

"Oh." His balloon of hope burst.

"I'll make you something delicious, though, don't worry." Sophie tilted her head toward the rabbits. "I really appreciate this. It's a great relief to find a home for those guys but—I have to go. My roast is due to come out of the oven."

"Wait here." Tanner drove his truck next to her van, loaded the rabbits and promised Beth she could come see them anytime. With Sophie's address tucked into his shirt pocket, he handed her one of Burt's cards with the phone number at Wranglers Ranch.

"So you can let me know when I should come and pick up the desserts," he said. Sophie nodded, fluttered a hand, then quickly drove away.

Chuckling at the goofy sunflower stuck on the van's rear bumper, Tanner started his engine.

Thanks to Sophie, his usher friends were going to get a surprise when they arrived at Wranglers Ranch tonight.

That's when it occurred to Tanner that he didn't even know if she was a good cook. For some reason that worry immediately dissipated. Strangely he felt utterly confident that whatever Sophie Armstrong made would be delicious. Tonight was going to be a good meeting.

Tanner gave the doughnut bag on his seat a glare, but he couldn't bring himself to throw it out. Living on the street in his teens, he'd felt that painful gnawing ache of hunger once too often to ever waste food. Spying a solution, he pulled a twenty-dollar bill from his wallet and handed it, the doughnuts and a business card to a disheveled man sitting in the parking lot by a light standard, exactly what Tanner would probably be doing if not for Burt Green.

"Hello. Buy yourself a meal to go with these doughnuts. If you need a job come see me at Wranglers Ranch," he said.

Tanner drove to the exit and left the city limits, marveling at the simplicity of the interaction. Maybe Burt's teaching wasn't totally wasted on him.

But that optimism faltered the closer Tanner got to Wranglers Ranch. Whom was he kidding? He didn't have the first clue how to carry out Burt's ideas for Wranglers even though the ranch had been his home for the past ten of his almost twenty-six years. Tanner had been thrilled to work alongside Burt, to share in helping the street kids he mentored, kids who wouldn't or couldn't fit into the institutions of Tucson. Foster parent Burt, with Social Services' permission, gladly nurtured each one, feeding, clothing and teaching life skills on his working ranch.

Ten years ago Tanner had been one of those kids. Other kids eventually found their families who'd missed them, wanted them back. Tanner was the only one who'd stayed. Nobody had ever come for him.

"Tanner, God's given me a new goal," Burt had announced last June. "I believe He wants us to make Wranglers Ranch into a kind of camp retreat for kids." The surprise of his words hadn't diminished even six months later.

Tanner might have been stunned by Burt's new goal but he'd never doubted his mentor would do it. He'd only been curious about how. Unfortunately a fatal heart attack had kept Burt from turning his goal into reality. Tanner had mourned his mentor, assuming Wranglers Ranch, which had been his home for so long, would be sold. He'd been stunned to learn that Burt had entrusted Tanner with his ranch and the fortune that went with it. Burt's will had just one condition: Tanner had two years to turn the ranch into a kids' camp. If he failed, then the ranch would be sold.

Tanner desperately wanted to live up to Burt's trust in him but he couldn't figure out how to make the dream happen. He had no difficulty running the ranch. That was easy. But the scope of creating a refuge for kids like the ones Burt had described overwhelmed and intimidated him. In six months he hadn't made even a tiny dent because he had no idea how to start. Shame over his failure left him feeling unworthy of Burt's trust. Failure meant he could never repay the enormous debt he owed the man who'd coaxed him off the streets and into a life in which faith in God now filled his world.

*Fan into flame the gift of God that is within you, Tanner.* In his mind he could hear Burt's voice repeating the verse from Timothy. Yet even now, after living at Wranglers so long, the meaning of that biblical quote still wasn't clear to Tanner.

*What is the gift that's within me, Burt?* Same old question. Still no answer.

Tanner knew he lacked Burt's easy ability to reach into a street kid's heart and help him gain a new perspective. He'd taken a foster parenting course and tons of psychology classes but they hadn't helped. He had the head knowledge. The problem was, Tanner Johns was a loner, plagued by his past mistakes.

The old insecurities returned as they always did when Tanner thought about his past. Once more he became a painfully shy seven-year-old foster kid, utterly devastated when he'd overheard a social worker say Tanner's mom abandoned him before he was a day old. In the years that followed he'd learned exactly what it meant when nobody wanted you, not even your own mother. From then on, a family was all Tanner had ever wanted. He'd finally found that family in Burt. But now he was gone and Tanner was alone.

Ignoring the rush of loss that bulged inside, Tanner pushed away the past and refocused. Even if he could somehow coax kids to come to the ranch, Burt's vision had been to turn Wranglers into a place where kids would find God was the answer to their problems. But how? Tanner had repeatedly asked God to send someone to show him. Then, as Burt had taught, he waited for God's leading. So far Tanner's prayers remained unanswered.

*Show me how to do this, God*, his heart cried once more.

With a sigh, Tanner turned his truck into the winding road that led to Wranglers, his spirit lifting at the beauty of the place. Burt had claimed the ranch showed its best in March and April when the desert bloomed with life. But January was Tanner's favorite month because it was a time of new birth, beginnings and hope.

The swaying leaves of the massive eucalyptus trees brought powerful memories of Burt and his unending life lessons. The only thing that wily man hadn't been able to teach Tanner was how to let go of his shameful past. Of course Burt hadn't known that by accepting his invitation to come to Wranglers, Tanner had abandoned the girlfriend who was going to have his child. In fact, it was only much later that Tanner himself understood that though he'd gained Burt and a home, he'd done exactly as his mother had—he'd thrown away his chance to be a father, to have the family he'd always craved. How could he possibly be forgiven for that?

With a sigh of regret Tanner pushed away the past and decided he'd focus on recruiting kids tomorrow. Right now he needed to relocate these rabbits so if a cute little girl, her grumpy brother and her pretty mom came to visit, he could allay their fears about their pets.

Moses Featherbed sat on the porch swing at Wranglers, watching as Tanner hefted the cage out of the truck. The elderly Native American had called Wranglers his home long before Tanner's arrival and thanks to a stipend from Burt's estate, Moses remained, refusing to retire, let alone stop rehabilitating the abused horses Burt had always welcomed on his spread.

"You raising rabbits now?" Moses, never short for a comment, lifted one bushy eyebrow.

"Not intentionally." Conscious of the old man following, Tanner carried the cage to a fenced area he'd built last November to house a pair of injured Canadian geese that had since flown away. "I made an exchange." He set the cage inside and opened the wire door.

"Rabbits for…?" Moses eased his arthritic hip onto a nearby bale and watched the animals hop out of the cage to explore their new home.

"Rabbits for pie or something like it for my ushers' meeting tonight." Tanner couldn't hide his smile of anticipation.

"Good deal, especially if a pretty lady comes with it," Moses approved with a chuckle.

"She's pretty all right," Tanner assured him. Then he frowned. "But that has nothing to do with the pie. I mean—uh—"

"Right." Moses's amused chuckle echoed through the feathery mesquites, over the spiky barrel cactus and tumbled down to the bubbling brook three hundred feet away. "The Lord's ways surely are mysterious."

Mysterious or not, the Lord wasn't in the matchmaking business for Tanner Johns, because pretty as Sophie Armstrong was, God knew perfectly well that Tanner didn't get involved with women. Never again.

"I sure hope your cowboy likes these kinds of pie." Sophie studied the fluted golden crusts with a critical eye.

"He will." Beth smiled dreamily, her mind obviously elsewhere. "Do you think the rabbits are happy, Mama?"

"On a ranch? I think they're ecstatic. That means very happy," she clarified when Beth frowned.

"Mr. Cowboy will be really nice to them." Beth went back to coloring her oversize rabbit-picture-thank-you card for the rancher.

"How do you know that?" Curious to hear the response, Sophie listened before completing a last-minute mental check on her catered meal.

"'Cause he was really nice to me. Only he's got sad eyes. I think he hurts inside. I don't think he has anybody to love him." Beth added a few blue lines to her drawing before she murmured, "*I* love him."

*I could almost love him for taking those rabbits.* Immediately Sophie quashed the errant thought. *Never falling into that trap again*, she reminded herself. *Independence is too precious.*

"I love Mr. Cowboy lots." Beth sounded the way Sophie had felt when she was fifteen and

Marty Armstrong, the coolest guy in school, had first shown an interest in her.

"That's nice to say, sweetie, but Mr. Johns is a stranger. You can't love a stranger." It was the wrong thing to say to her very literal daughter, and Sophie knew it the moment Beth's blue eyes darkened to storm clouds.

"The Bible says to love everybody." She glared at her mother, her voice accusing.

"That's right. Thank you for reminding me, Bethy." Sophie pressed a placating kiss against her daughter's head, then checked the kitchen clock. Where was the man? She had to leave for her gig in less than five minutes. "Maybe that's him," she said when the phone rang a second later.

It wasn't Tanner Johns calling.

"I can't babysit, Sophie. I'm so sorry." Edna Parker's breathy voice sounded horribly weak.

"What's wrong, Edna? Where are you?" Sophie asked worriedly.

"At the hospital. My son brought me. I fell and broke my hip while you were out trying to get rid of the rabbits. They're going to do surgery soon." That weepy tone told Sophie her elderly neighbor was very frightened.

"You stop fussing now," she said gently. "The doctors will make everything better."

"But I can't babysit for you tonight," the woman wailed in a feeble voice.

"I'll get someone else to watch the kids. Don't worry about us. And I'll run over later and look after your cats. I have your key, remember? Everything's going to be fine." She heard a sigh of relief. "The kids and I will come see you as soon as we can. Don't worry, Edna."

"Thank you, dear." Somewhat calmer, Edna chatted for a moment before saying, "I'm so glad God sent you into my life." Then she hung up.

"I wish God would send me someone into *my* life. Where am I going to get a sitter at this time on a Friday night?" Sophie couldn't mess up this catering job. She needed it to pay next month's rent. "I need help, God."

A loud rap on the front door startled her out of her silent prayer.

"It's Mr. Cowboy," Beth yelled, having raced to answer the door. Then to Sophie's utter dismay, her daughter said to Tanner, "Houston, we have a problem."

Tanner's startled gaze moved from Beth to Sophie. One corner of his mouth kicked up. Dark green eyes, which earlier had been hidden behind sunglasses, were startling in his tanned face. Sophie gulped. Tall, lanky and lean, with wide denim-clad shoulders that looked perfect for leaning on, Tanner Johns was every woman's fantasy cowboy.

Not *her* fantasy cowboy, of course, but—

"What's the problem, er, Houston?" His gaze rested on Sophie while his fingers gripped the black Stetson he'd removed when he stepped over their threshold.

Sophie couldn't explain because there was something wrong with her breathing. As in, she couldn't. Then Davy came racing down the stairs, tripped on the perpetually loose runner at the bottom tread and tumbled headlong into the cowboy's arms. Tanner grunted as he caught her son and held on just long enough to make sure Davy could stand on his own.

"Something I said?" he joked, winking at her.

The man *winked* at her! The control Sophie had almost recovered vanished. She figured she probably looked like a beached fish, gulping for air. Stupidly, she wished she'd had time to fix her hair.

*Where's your independence now?*

"Our babysitter can't come," Beth explained. "Mama's gonna lose this job and we need it to pay our bills." The words were an exact repeat of her mother's earlier meant-to-be-silent mutterings.

Sophie almost groaned out loud. Tanner so needed to hear that sad story, he of the billion-acre ranch with money coming out of his ears, thanks, according to church gossip, to Burt's generosity. Now he'd feel sorry for her. Sophie thrust back her shoulders, independence reasserting itself.

"That's enough, Beth. You and Davy get your sweaters. You'll have to come with me and sit quietly in a corner of the kitchen while I work. Go now. Monica and Tiffany will meet us there." She said hello to Tanner and beckoned him to follow her to the kitchen.

"Monica and Tiffany?" he said in a dazed voice. "You have more children?"

"They're my catering helpers." Sophie pointed. "Your pies."

When there was no response, she paused in lifting the pan holding her perfectly sliced roast from the oven to look at him. Her heart gave a bump of pure sympathy. The poor man was gazing at her pies as if he hadn't eaten for months. So maybe his massive inheritance couldn't buy everything, but she had no time to think about that now.

"Tanner?" She said it more crisply than she intended. He lost the hungry look and snapped to attention. "Sorry to rush you. You'll have to wrap them yourself. The foil's over there. I've got to load up and get going."

"I'll help you." He took the heavy metal server from her and insisted she lead him to the garage where the van was open, waiting. He stored the container where she indicated, then carried out the other dishes, refusing to let her lift even one though she assured him she'd done it many times before.

"Thank you for your help," Sophie said when everything was placed so it couldn't move during the trip. "Now I must leave. Beth. Davy," she called.

"Aw, Mom. Do I have to go?" Her son glared at her. "I'm not a baby, you know."

"I know you're growing up fast, but you're still too young to stay alone. Now please come on. I don't have time to waste arguing." Too aware of Tanner standing next to her, Sophie reached out to grab her son's arm to draw him forward.

"I could take your children back to the ranch with me while you work."

The cowboy's offer stunned her. It must have stunned him, too, because Tanner gawked at her, green eyes stretched wide as if he was in shock.

"It's very kind of you to offer but you're a stranger," she said as nicely as she could. If only she could accept. It would save— What was she thinking? It was impossible.

"There will be eleven other men at the meeting. One will be Pastor Jeff and at least two others are church board members. You can call any of them for references if you want." Tanner waited.

Could he know how desperately she wanted to accept his offer? "Please let me help," he murmured when she'd wasted several more moments. "These pies—you've no idea what they mean to me. I'd like to return the favor, if you'll let me."

"You already did by taking the rabbits," Sophie reminded. He only smiled and waited, watching her with that intense contemplation that had turned more hazel now that flecks of copper glinted in the depths.

"Can we go to his ranch, Mom?" Davy's hopeful voice broke the silence.

"What about your meeting?" Sophie knew Davy wouldn't settle while she was working, and that would disturb Beth, which would distract her. She desperately needed tonight's job to go right. Dare she risk leaving her kids with this man?

"I draw up the usher schedules ahead of time. It's just a matter of everyone confirming dates and then sampling your pie." Tanner's grin made her stomach swoop so she felt off balance. "It's an excuse for guy time. Your kids won't be an issue, Sophie. Moses will make sure of that."

As Tanner explained to the kids about a Native American man who lived at the ranch, Sophie could no longer resist his offer. She lifted her cell phone from her pocket and dialed the pastor's number. Once she'd laid out the situation, Pastor Jeff gave his wholehearted reassurance.

"Tanner's a great guy, Sophie. He's going to turn Burt's ranch into a kind of outreach camp. I'm hoping our church can partner with him." His effusive praise for the rancher went on and on. When she didn't immediately respond, Jeff said, "If you're still worried, know that I'll be there to make sure nothing happens to Beth and Davy."

"I appreciate that, Jeff." She ended the call, closed the phone, then looked at Tanner. "Thank you, I'd like to accept your offer."

He nodded and turned away, probably to hide the embarrassed flush rising up his neck. Sophie regretted causing that but she had to be sure the kids would be safe. She drew Davy aside and stared him straight in the eye.

"Same rules as at home, buddy. You don't go anywhere on the ranch if Tanner isn't there. You obey him and Moses without question. If I hear one word—"

"You won't." Davy eagerly grabbed his jacket and held out his sister's. "Come on, Bethy. We're going to a real ranch."

Davy's use of the old pet name for his sister made Sophie smile. His good mood probably wouldn't last, but while it did she'd enjoy it.

It took only minutes to store the now-covered pies in the side boxes of Tanner's truck, minutes more to kiss her babies and promise to pick them up as soon as she was finished working. Sophie searched her brain, worried she'd missed something, forgotten something important.

"Go do your job, Sophie." Tanner's quiet reassurance brought back the reality of time. "I promise I'll keep Beth and Davy safe for you."

"Thank you," she said sincerely. A moment later, with her kids safely belted into their seats, Tanner drove away and Sophie left home with her meal, clinging to her wobbly faith that this time God would be there for her.

She'd almost forgotten the Sunday she'd been on cleanup duty after a potluck at the church and overheard Burt speaking to someone about Tanner.

"He had a rough childhood and his teen years weren't much better. His past dogs him. But there isn't a man I trust more than Tanner Johns. His integrity, honesty and uprightness are part of what makes him tick."

The old man must have truly trusted Tanner to bequeath his beloved Wranglers Ranch to him. Burt's latest dream for the place was something the whole congregation had learned about from a presentation he'd made a few weeks before his death. The reason Sophie remembered that specific conversation, though, was because of Burt's last words.

*"As I keep telling Tanner, we must fan into flame the gift of God inside us."*

So, Sophie wondered, what was Tanner's gift? Knight in shining armor?

The mental image of him riding a white steed, or in this case his white truck, to her rescue made Sophie blush. She got back to work forcing away that image and the memory of the way her senses had reacted to the big cowboy, especially to that slow, easy smile of his. She'd been this route before with Marty, and life had been a painful teacher.

Her husband Marty's greatest attraction had been his charm. He'd been as big a kid as his own children, fun-loving, living for the moment, never giving a thought to tomorrow, often to the detriment of his family. In the two years since his death Sophie had finally put her life back together and regained control. Sure, every day was a struggle to make ends meet, but it was *her* struggle, *her* bank account to hide away for real emergencies. *She* was the person she depended on. No way was she giving up her independence or security now.

Sophie wasn't ever going to be dependent on any man again, even if he was a big strong cowboy with a smile that made a zillion butterflies skip in her stomach.

# Chapter Two

"I'm afraid I wore out your kids." Tanner liked the way Sophie's upswept hair left her graceful neck free for his inspection.

"I hope they behaved." Three and a half hours later the cook's black fitted blouse and slacks still looked pristine. In fact, Sophie appeared relaxed and calm, exactly the type of competent professional you'd want catering your occasion. "Davy..."

"Loves horses. I could barely keep him from saddling up. His enthusiasm is great." Tanner chuckled at her surprise. "No kidding. He's a natural cowboy. They're sleeping in the other room. Want to check?" She nodded so he led the way.

Sophie's lovely face softened when she saw Beth curled in Burt's chair in front of the fire next to Davy, who'd thrown his arm across her shoulder in a protective manner. Tanner pointed to the kitchen and after a long moment she nodded and followed.

"Thank you," Sophie said quietly.

"They're good kids. After my meeting ended I took them out to feed the rabbits. They approve of the bunnies' new home." He smiled at her eye roll. "How did the job go?"

"Perfectly. I have just enough beef left over to make us a stew tomorrow and not a spoonful remains of my chocolate cherry trifle." Despite the lines of weariness around her eyes, Sophie looked happy. "And I have two new jobs."

"Great." He motioned to the stove. "Do you have time for tea? I just made a pot."

"I'd love a cup. Thank you." Sophie sank into the chair he offered. "Somehow I didn't see you as a tea drinker."

"Burt only drank coffee in the morning. He refused to make it after that. Since my coffee is worse than mud it was easier to drink whatever he made. It's pretty hard even for me to mess up tea bags." He poured tea into two mugs before realizing he should have used the good cups. "I have some pie left. Would you like a slice?"

"No, thanks. I like making pie but eating it is bad for my waist." Sophie frowned at him. "Which kinds were left?"

"One apple and one strawberry rhubarb." He sat down across from her thinking that there was nothing wrong with her waist. "Don't make that face. It wasn't because they didn't like them," he reassured her. "They did. I knew most of them would take seconds or thirds so I hid two pieces before they got here."

She frowned. "Why?"

"Because I wanted some for tomorrow." He shrugged when she grinned. "Self-preservation. You make very good pies."

"Thank you but I'm sure your housekeeper keeps you well fed." Sophie's gaze moved around the kitchen.

"I don't have a housekeeper. The hands are all married and eat at home. Moses prefers his own cooking. It's just me." She looked dubious. "It's true. When he was alive, Burt did the cooking or we ate out."

"What a shame with a kitchen like this. It's a cook's dream." A soft yearning look filled Sophie's face as she studied the stainless steel appliances. "You have every piece of equipment any cook could dream of."

"Probably." He shrugged carelessly. "Burt had this room redone several months ago and then asked the Public Health Department to certify it as commercial. He hoped to use it for meal preparation when he got the camps going."

"When will that be?" Sophie leaned back in

her chair, mug in hand, and let the steam bathe her face.

"Good question." Tanner forced himself to stop staring at her and admitted, "I'm struggling to get things started because I don't have Burt's gift for striking up conversations with kids. I'm not even sure how to start a camp or whatever for them. Actually I'm scared witless at the thought of hosting a group of troubled kids for a whole week, but that was Burt's goal."

"Why must you start with a full-week camp?" Sophie tilted her head, her face thoughtful. "Couldn't you try a one-day riding camp first, maybe get some practice at running that before you branch out?"

Tanner blinked. He'd been overwhelmed by the scope of Burt's impossible dream, but this smaller step seemed feasible.

"How do you see that working?" He waited with a wiggle of excitement flaring inside, for Sophie to expand on her idea.

"Hmm. Maybe the kids would arrive Saturday morning between seven and eight? You could have a buffet breakfast while they assemble. Kids are always hungry." She smiled, her full lips tipping up in a way that set his heart thudding. "After that they could mingle among the horses."

"That way we could assess their skills without being too obvious." Logical and organized.

Tanner liked that about Sophie. "Also they could get to know their ride. But we'd need some time to prepare the horses," he mused with a frown.

"So maybe a little explanation about the horses while you prepare. After that you tell them the rules for the trail ride and what to expect." Sophie glanced at him, eyebrows lifted in a question. "Then you mount up."

"And just ride?" He thought that sounded boring.

"You could break up the ride." Sophie didn't laugh or mock him for his lack of ideas. Instead she chewed on her bottom lip, a frown marring her smooth forehead as she thought it through. "Maybe you'd stop along the way to explain about the desert, the animals that live here, talk about Wranglers Ranch and how it came to be—stuff like that."

"That'd be Moses's job," Tanner said, thinking how easily her plan came together. "He knows everything there is to know about this spread and the desert adjoining us."

"Perfect." Her smile made him feel as if he could handle this.

Suddenly Tanner didn't find Burt's dream quite so daunting.

"At the end of the ride you might have a campfire picnic or maybe a chuck wagon dinner." Sophie studied him, assessing his response. "Doable?"

"Sure. We could follow that with stories, maybe bring up God's creation," Tanner added thoughtfully. "It's a good plan. A small group would give us a chance to do a trial run, iron out problems."

"It wouldn't be hard to turn that into a two-day camp, either, if you had somewhere on the ranch for people to camp out overnight. Breakfast in the desert, ride back to the ranch for lunch, then head home. It sounds—" Sophie's smile faltered. "You're frowning."

"Because I don't see how this plan attracts street kids." Tanner avoided her gaze. "They were Burt's primary focus."

"Maybe to get there you have to start with other kids," Sophie said in a thoughtful voice. "Maybe if you got a buzz going about this place, street kids would come out of curiosity. There are lots of needy kids who could benefit from coming here. Building a rapport with a horse and the people who care for them could be a bridge to reaching many kids."

"You think?" Tanner hadn't considered that.

"Sure. I'd enroll Davy in a program like that if it was available and I could afford it." Sophie set her cup down and placed her hands in her lap. Her voice dropped. "Actually I'm willing to try almost anything to engage him. He's not yet nine but he's already gotten in with a bad bunch of kids. His behavior and attitude are suffering at school, too. I'm his mother but I feel like I'm failing him."

"I sincerely doubt that." Tanner didn't think a caring mom like her would ever disappoint her child or abandon him as his own mother had.

"I homeschool Beth and that takes a lot of prep time, but I have to do it. She just wasn't progressing at her school." Sophie sighed. "By necessity she gets a lot of attention from me. So does my job and when I've finished that—"

"You're wiped out," he completed, seeing the weariness in her posture.

"Yes." Sophie's head drooped. "And Davy suffers. His 'friends' have already persuaded him to steal a candy bar. I reprimanded and punished him but I'm worried about what comes next. I don't know what to do. I'm doing the best I can but…"

Tanner had to say something to erase the misery on her face.

"Davy was great tonight. He even offered to help Moses muck out stalls." He grinned as astonishment filled Sophie's face. "Don't worry, I didn't let him. I said we'd need your permission first, but Davy is definitely intrigued by the animals. He went from tough bravado to quiet gentleness in about three seconds flat when he met an abused horse someone dropped off today."

"My son—gentle?" Sophie's big brown eyes stretched wide. "Davy?"

"Davy," Tanner affirmed. He liked her honesty about her son. "Maybe that's an interest you can build on, which is also why this idea of yours could be worthwhile." His brain whirled with ideas. "If Wranglers helped only Davy it would at least be a step toward making Burt's dream come true."

"Doing that means a lot to you?" she said softly.

"It's the only reason I accepted his legacy of Wranglers. I have less than two years left to turn Burt's dream into reality. Maybe a day camp is the way to finally start down that path." Tanner grabbed a pen and pad of paper from near the phone. "For me the biggest issue will be the food. Hey!" He grinned at her. "Could we hire you to cook?"

"I'd need to check dates but I'm sure we could work out something." Sophie didn't look at him as she asked, "Maybe I could cook in lieu of Davy's fee to attend?"

"We could talk about that." Tanner saw hurt flicker through her eyes when he didn't immediately accept and mentally kicked himself for causing it. But his strong reactions to this woman scared him. He didn't want to encourage anything that could be construed as personal with her. Or anyone else. "I need to keep everything business-like," he excused quickly.

"Of course. So do I." The hurt look disappeared as she nodded. "Profit and loss to make it official. Then when you've done several camps you'll have built a résumé that you can use for schools or public agencies so they'll see you're not just playing at this. Good idea."

It hadn't been his idea at all. It was hers. And a good one at that.

"Thank you for understanding, Sophie. But I would like to have Davy attend the first camp." He saw her surprise. *Don't say anything about what he did. Don't get involved*, his brain ordered. Too late.

"Why?" Sophie's gaze narrowed. "Because you feel sorry for him?"

"Sorry?" How could he phrase this without offending her? "No. I see Davy as sort of a guinea pig. Maybe I should say 'test subject.'" Sophie's dark eyes narrowed so Tanner hurried to clarify. "If Davy was part of the first ride, I could question him afterward and see from his perspective where we missed a need or should do something differently. I wouldn't want to ask a guest those kinds of questions. But if Davy was part of my team—" He saw skepticism in her intelligent gaze. "You don't want that."

"I think it's wonderful of you and he'd love it,

I'm sure." The frown furrowing her forehead returned. What a concerned mother she was. "But what if he does something he shouldn't? What if he messes up?"

*He already has.*

"Then we'll learn from that, too." Tanner smiled at her. Somehow it seemed important to reach this boy. At least he could do that, couldn't he? "Davy's a little kid. What could happen?"

"You'd be surprised." A wry tilt of her lips told Tanner Sophie's equanimity was returning. "Okay, but I hope you don't regret this idea. You do realize Davy doesn't know how to ride."

"So we'll teach him." Tanner shrugged to show her it was no big deal. Suddenly he wanted to know more about Sophie. "Your husband must have been glad of your quick thinking." Immediately shutters dropped over her eyes, telling him it was the wrong thing to say. "That's private. I'm sorry."

"No, it's fine." She huffed out a sigh and then sipped her tea. Just when he thought she would get up and leave, Sophie lifted her head and looked him in the eye. "I guess Marty did depend on me. He certainly didn't have a head for business."

"Is Davy like him?" Tanner asked, curious about the man this lovely woman had married.

"I hope not." Sophie smiled at his startled look.

"I loved my husband but he wasn't what you'd call responsible. Marty was like a big kid, carefree, enjoying himself without worrying about the future."

"Tough on you," he murmured.

"Yes. I was the heavy, the one who said no to his wilder ideas, and Davy was old enough to see that." Sophie's pretty face tightened at the memory. "I'm trying to teach my son that responsibility is part of growing up, that nobody gets out of it."

"Is that what Marty tried to do, get out of his responsibility?" It was none of Tanner's business but he had to ask. His stomach knotted when Sophie slowly nodded. What would she think if she knew of his past irresponsibility? "How did Marty die?"

Normally Tanner would have steered far away from such personal questions. But here, in the intimacy of his kitchen, he had a strange feeling that Sophie wanted to share her past and that she needed to talk to someone. He'd guess she didn't do that often but maybe with her kids asleep and her job finished, she could finally relax. She'd helped him. He wanted to help her.

"I'm a good listener, Sophie," he assured her quietly. Silence yawned.

"Marty died riding bulls at the rodeo."

It wasn't so much those seven words as the way

Sophie said them that told Tanner how much her husband's decision to take that risk had affected her. He made no comment, simply waited for her to continue.

"Beth was three months old and our medical bills were huge. Marty was looking for an easy way to pay them off." She bowed her head as if ashamed about her debt. "The rodeo purse was a large amount. Marty being Marty never considered it was so large because no one could ride the animal, or that he might get hurt trying. After three seconds, the bull threw him, then trampled him. Marty was unconscious for four days before he died."

Leaving Sophie with even larger medical bills and no one to help her. Irritation toward the careless husband built with a rush of—what? Not pity. Sympathy? Compassion—that was it. And a wish that he'd been there to help her. But why was that? Tanner was a loner. He barely knew Sophie Armstrong. So why should he feel she needed his help?

"That must have been very hard for you, alone with a newborn and another child." A thousand questions bubbled inside him. "What did you do?"

"I cried for a while but that was useless so I grabbed control of my life." Sophie's voice hardened. "I felt like I'd lost it in high school when I learned I was pregnant with Davy. My parents were furious their daughter had strayed from the Christian path." Her voice showed the strain of that time. "They insisted Marty and I get married. I obeyed them even though I had a lot of doubts about marriage and motherhood at sixteen."

"Sixteen? Wow. That is young." Tanner gulped down the memory of his own life at sixteen and the mistake he was still running from, the thing that made him utterly unworthy of Burt's trust or anyone's love. "When Marty died, did you contact your parents?"

"His and mine both, to tell them of his death. I could have used my parents' support then but I couldn't take their recriminations." Sophie's usually laughing lips tightened. "My parents are big into rules and judgment. I didn't need the guilt of hearing about how my sins were coming back to roost."

"His parents couldn't help, either?" Sophie shook her head. "So you were alone. How did you survive?" Tanner was aghast that this young woman had faced life as the sole support for two very young children.

"Marty had an insurance policy. I got it the day he bought a house that was beyond our means. The policy paid off our mortgage but we couldn't afford to live there so I sold the place and everything else we didn't absolutely need." Sophie's chin thrust out as if she expected some argument from Tanner, as if she'd had to justify her decision before.

Tanner remained silent, amazed at her pluck and grit.

"That money, a cleaning job with a neighbor babysitting for free and the food bank gave us a cushion while I figured out my next step." She shrugged. "People liked my cooking so I started selling it at farmers' markets to make a few dollars extra. That grew into catering and eventually allowed me to stay home with Beth. We manage now."

"So you have your own business." Tanner felt enormously proud of Sophie and he barely knew her!

"It hasn't been easy, but yes, I love being my own boss." She grimaced. "Along the way I've struggled to figure out God's plan but—hey, that's enough of my life story."

"Thank you for sharing it with me," Tanner said and meant it. "You're a remarkable woman, Sophie Armstrong."

"I'm just a mom trying to do the very best for my kids. They come first." She said it with a fierce purpose, her eyes dark with determination. "Davy and Beth are why I keep pushing through the problems. My kids are my life. I will never knowingly endanger them. I will also never again allow my life to be controlled by someone else."

Sophie's darkened eyes and stern voice brooked no argument. Her harsh life had obviously strengthened her but Tanner hated to see the tiny fan lines of stress at the sides of her eyes.

"So now you believe Davy needs to learn responsibility?" He waited for her nod, feeling slightly guilty for thinking he had something he could teach this boy, he who had abdicated fatherhood of his own child. "How will you teach him that?" he asked curiously.

"By finding something he loves and then indulging it as much as I can afford. Maybe he'll begin to understand that some things are worth working for." Her firm clear voice and focused gaze told him Sophie needed no greater motivation for her life than her kids.

How Tanner admired that motherly devotion. "And Beth? What does she need?"

"Beth—" Sophie paused, her face momentarily reflective. "Beth will be fine." Her dark eyes softened and the hard thrust of her jaw relaxed. "She takes whatever life hands her and turns it into a rainbow. She's adaptable. Davy's different." Her lips pinched tight. "He needs something…more."

"God certainly knew what He was doing when He made you their mother." Tanner was positive he'd never known anyone more determined than

Sophie Armstrong. He noted her quick glance at the wall clock, saw it swerve to rest on Beth's card sitting on a shelf. Her smile returned. "It's a pretty card," he said. "More tea?"

"No, thanks. I must get home." She rose, set her cup in the sink then faced him. "I can't thank you enough for helping me out tonight, Tanner."

"I think four pies more than covered that bill. This ranch will have a new reputation at church thanks to you. The best eats ever at Wranglers Ranch." He grinned and when she smiled back he decided Sophie's pies weren't the best thing about her. Her smile was.

Silence yawned between them. Tanner's gaze locked with hers and he couldn't look away from those intense brown eyes until Sophie's cough snapped the electrical current running between them.

"I need to go," she said again. "But if I can somehow help with your project here at Wranglers, I hope you'll tell me."

"Thanks." How generous to make such a gracious offer with all she had on her plate. "I will."

She nodded once before she stepped around him and walked into the living room. "Come on, guys. Time to get home."

Tanner watched in silent admiration as Sophie gently shook Davy's shoulder, then Beth's, wakening them in a tender loving tone. The children roused easily, yawning as they straightened.

"We had the bestest time, Mama. Thank you, Cowboy Tanner." Beth insisted on calling him *Cowboy.* Tanner liked it. It made him feel as if he was somehow more noteworthy than the men she usually encountered. He basked in her sweet smile.

"You're welcome, Beth. I hope you come again." Tanner surprised himself with the invitation. Sophie's presence here made his pulse speed up, and that made him nervous. He was all about not getting involved, yet there was something about Sophie and her little family that drew him, made him want to interact with them again.

"Hey, Mom." Davy was fully awake now and full of information. "Bethy was telling Tanner how you homeschool her and how you're the leader."

"I'm just chairman of the homeschool association," Sophie corrected gently.

"Whatever. Anyway I remembered you said you have to arrange an outing for the homeschool kids." He grinned at his sister. "Beth and me think coming to Wranglers Ranch would be fun. I could come, too. To help," he added, his chest puffed out.

Tanner hadn't encouraged Davy when he'd posed the thought earlier, and he was glad he hadn't because a doubtful look washed over Sophie's face as she glanced from her son to him.

"You'd be a big help, son. But I don't know about visiting a ranch. Not all the homeschool kids can ride horses. What would they do out here?" she asked.

"There's tons of stuff to do." Davy grinned at Tanner. "This old guy, Moses, knows all about the original settlers and the Indians that lived here first. He tells lots of cool stories."

"And the horses need people to feed and brush them," Beth added. "I got to pet a white one. It's called Jeremiah, right?" she asked Tanner, who nodded.

"I'd rather ride Gideon. He looks like he's fast." Davy's eyes glowed with excitement.

"Moses, Jeremiah and Gideon. Sounds like you've got an Old Testament theme going at Wranglers Ranch." Sophie smiled at Tanner.

My, how he liked that smile.

"Burt's idea. Every time he read a passage about a Bible character's struggles, he'd figure out how he could apply that lesson to his own life. Then he'd use the hero's name on a rescued horse to remind himself." Tanner nodded. "We have Melchizedek, Ehud, Balaam—want me to continue?"

"I get the idea. Old Testament heroes." She rolled her eyes.

"And heroines. Burt was an equal opportunity *namer*." Tanner couldn't smother his laughter when Sophie's face twisted in a droll look. "No kidding. We have Rhoda, Abishag and Bathsheba to name a few."

"Abishag?" Sophie's chortles lifted the gloom that had settled over the house since Burt's passing. Tanner felt as if the joyful sound swept the house free of grief and loss and replaced it with— hope?

"Maybe you haven't read about her. Abishag was a beautiful young woman who was chosen to marry David in his old age and cherish him." Tanner shrugged. "I'm not sure what Burt's lesson about her was but there must have been one because he chose that name for a mare."

"Abishag is a really pretty horse. She has black and white spots." Davy turned to Tanner. "What kind did you say?"

"A pinto," he said, then fell silent as the children regaled their mother with all the things they'd done with Tanner.

"Okay, odd names aside," Sophie said when they finally ran out of stories, "since my kids are so impressed with Wranglers Ranch, maybe you and I *should* have a discussion about arranging for the homeschool kids to come here. This sounds like a great place to visit."

Davy cheered so loudly the dog started to yowl.

"Sheba, quiet." Tanner tried to shush the excited animal.

"Sheba." Sophie slid her arm around each child's shoulder. "As in queen of—?" She arched one dark eyebrow in a question.

"Everything." Tanner laughed at her groan. It was such fun teasing with Sophie. He walked with her as she shepherded her family out to her van, waited till they were all buckled in, then leaned toward the driver's open window. "I really appreciate those pies, Sophie. And I hope you'll come again soon. Your homeschool kids are also welcome if they want to visit."

"I'll see what the rest of the board thinks. They might want to visit your ranch first." She frowned. "Would that be a problem?"

"Not at all, but you should give me a heads-up before you come," he said quickly. He liked to be prepared, get his barriers up, Burt would have said. "We're working on replacement fencing up in the hills and I'm not always here."

"Okay." Was Sophie's hesitation because she was as loath to leave as he was to have her go? "See you."

*I hope so.*

He nodded and waved. When the van's red taillights disappeared around the bend, Tanner let his hand fall to his side, marveling at how alone it suddenly felt in this place that had been his home for so long, the place he enjoyed particularly *because of* the solitude. Tonight he'd welcome company to stop him from thinking about Sophie, but Moses had disappeared to his little cottage after the kids had fallen asleep.

Tanner walked back inside Burt's home, then jerked to a stop, suddenly seeing the rooms through new eyes. The updated modernity of the stainless steel kitchen and pristinely tiled bathroom didn't match the worn and shabby masculinity of the living room. Whenever possible Tanner avoided sitting in Burt's leather chair, the place where the kids had slept, because it had a spring that hit him in exactly the wrong spot. And it was becoming increasingly difficult to get comfortable on the stained and sagging plaid sofa, which was far too tattered to be restored by simple cleaning.

Tanner kept the place as tidy as he could, but tonight, through Sophie's eyes, he wondered who in their right mind had chosen the dreary red-and-black wallpaper, which in no way went with the horrible mud-brown carpet that was alternately matted in places and threadbare in others. There was no warm, cozy feeling here, not like at Sophie's home.

He thought about her suggestions for a day camp, which in his opinion had real merit. But if he pursued it there could be occasions when groups would have to come inside, say if it was raining or too windy outside. Burt had worked hard on the exterior appearance of Wranglers Ranch because he wanted those who visited to see his ranch in top-notch condition. Shouldn't that include the inside of the house, as well?

This room definitely didn't say "welcome." Tanner didn't have a clue how to achieve a hospitable feel, but he figured there were people in Tucson who did. He'd told Sophie he'd be working on fences, but his ranch hands were more than capable of doing that. He went along only in hopes the open spaces would help him figure out how to make Burt's dream live. Instead Sophie had showed him how to start.

Tanner went back to the kitchen, grabbed his Bible from a shelf and sat down, prepared to ask God about his next move. Immediately his nose caught Sophie's citrusy fragrance and his brain framed her laughing face.

Would she come back to Wranglers? Soon?

And why did it matter so much?

# Chapter Three

Two weeks later Sophie ended her morning visit at the hospital after praying for added strength for Edna.

She thought God would answer that prayer because of Edna's strong faith in Him. But as she drove to Wranglers Ranch, Sophie couldn't bring herself to ask Him to affirm her decision to return to the ranch and the man she couldn't stop thinking about. She just couldn't trust that God would help her get over this silly attraction to a real-life cowboy.

"Do you think Cowboy Tanner missed us?" Beth asked from the backseat, completely ignoring Sophie's advice to stick with plain Tanner. "Bertie's mom told Cora Lee's mom that it was about time you got us a new daddy. Are we getting a new daddy, Mama?"

"No, honey, we're not." Sophie forced herself

to unclench her jaw. Why did Beth's best friend have to be the son of the block's biggest gossip?

*I am not interested in Tanner Johns.*

Her brain laughed. Okay so she hadn't been very successful at banishing a host of mental images of the rancher and his lazy smile. But nobody needed to know that, especially Bertie's mom.

"I want to ask you something, honey," she said, changing the subject quickly.

"Okay." Beth nodded. Her blue eyes sparkled with excitement. "Is it a secret, like what Bertie's mom said?" She frowned. "Maybe I wasn't supposed to tell what she said."

"Oh, that wasn't a secret," Sophie reassured her with a mental grimace. The whole block probably knew about Tanner now. "Listen, Bethy. I need to have an important talk with Tanner and I don't want you to interrupt. I brought your crayons so you can color while we talk."

"Okay." Her daughter smoothed out the skirt of the dress Sophie had made her. There'd been no talking Beth out of wearing what was meant to be her Sunday best to the ranch today. Beth had a big crush on her Cowboy Tanner. Like mother, like daughter? "Can I see the rabbits, Mama?"

"If you don't interrupt, maybe you can see

them when we're finished." Sophie frowned. "Do you understand?"

"Only interrupt if it's important," Beth promised.

Of course, Beth's *important* never meant what it did to others, but Sophie knew it was the best she could hope for. Talking about it more now that they were arriving would only confuse her daughter. She turned the corner, frowning as she noticed a group of people scattered all over the front yard. Some sat on the patchy grass, sipping from cans of soda, while others carried stuff from a big delivery truck. What was going on?

She parked her van in what she hoped was an out-of-the-way place, then she and Beth walked toward the door. Tanner met them, his grin wide and welcoming.

"This is a bad time for you," Sophie said, dismayed because she knew Beth wouldn't settle with so many people around. Even now she was chattering a mile a minute to a man she'd never met. "You should have put me off. I need to talk to you but it isn't urgent."

"There's no problem," he said easily. "Hey, Beth." He smiled at her daughter, admired her dress, then turned back to Sophie. "They're almost finished with the deliveries. Just taking a break while the designer rearranges a few things."

Designer? For a place for street kids?

*Stop judging, Sophie.*

"We can come back another time if it works better," she offered.

"Actually I was hoping you'd take a look while you're here and tell me what you think of my changes," he said with obvious eagerness. "Come on in. You, too, Beth." He took the little girl's hand and led her inside.

This was not the entry Sophie had used last time, but it led directly into the same room where her kids had fallen asleep. Only it wasn't the same. The dowdy old room had been transformed with the addition of a bank of windows facing north.

"It's so pretty, Mr. Cowboy." Beth's eyes were huge.

"Brilliant idea to make the windows floor to ceiling." Sophie was astounded by the light flooding the room.

"They're actually doors." Tanner showed her how one door folded against the other until the entire wall was open. "The workmen out there are creating a stone patio with lots of seating, including around a fireplace."

So Tanner was using Bert's fortune for himself. A flicker of disappointment wiggled through her but Sophie shrugged it off. Why did it matter to her that he was making his living quarters more comfortable? This room had been ugly and desperately in need of a face-lift. Tanner had the funds and there was nothing wrong with modernizing.

"I'm sure it will be lovely," she murmured.

"Actually you gave me the idea," he said, shocking her.

"Me?" Sophie blinked. "I said nothing about redecorating."

"No, but after all you said about day camps I got thinking how this room would be a great place to bring guests if it was raining or something. That grew into 'why not have a patio area, partly covered, where people could relax after their ride?' Or it could be for entertaining. I might have to do that if we get groups—" He paused. "I don't think you approve, Sophie," he said with a frown. "Is it the furniture? Maybe leather sofas are too much, but the designer said they're the easiest to clean if someone spills. I've heard kids usually spill."

"Yes, they do." She couldn't get over the difference he'd made. The room was warm and welcoming, inviting conversations in any of the casual groupings scattered around the big open space. Pale cream walls left no indication that redbird wallpaper—they had been birds, hadn't they?—had once nested there.

"You think I wasted Burt's money." He sank onto the arm of a sofa, his face defeated. "Maybe

I did. I hemmed and hawed over this decision a lot." His tone grew somber. "It kept me awake thinking how many meals all this could buy for someone on the street."

Sophie tried to mask her feelings. "But you went ahead anyway."

"Yes, because of something Moses said." A funny look flickered across Tanner's ruggedly handsome face. "He asked me if I'd rather eat in a dump or a palace."

"That makes sense." But Sophie wasn't swayed. She'd heard the same kind of rationalization from Marty too many times.

"Moses helped me realize that people who've known toughness and hurt appreciate comfort just as much as the rest of us. I want everyone who comes to Burt's ranch to be comfortable." He rose slowly. "I'm sorry you don't approve."

"Oh, Tanner." Sophie hated that she'd spoiled his happiness. She touched his arm, wishing she hadn't immediately thought the worst of him. Independence was a fine thing but it was time to realize that not every man was like Marty. "I didn't say I didn't approve."

"You didn't have to." He seemed disappointed, his earlier joy gone. "It's in your face and your voice."

"I was just surprised. Anyone would love to come here. You've created a very comfortable, beautiful place." Sophie smiled at him. "I'm overwhelmed by the change. It's so different."

"Thanks." He looked relieved. "I particularly wanted this room perfect because further down the line, when things are more established, I hope to invite Social Services or some organization like that to come see what Wranglers can offer kids." He made a face. "I doubt they'd be impressed by the former decor. If they one day agree to partner in a program for needy children, I want this place to be ready."

"You've changed, also." Sophie studied the bright glint in his green eyes. "When we talked before you seemed as if you were struggling to begin Burt's dream but now you're charging ahead full speed." It wasn't a criticism. More that she couldn't quite define the change she saw in him.

"Because of you. You planted ideas that wouldn't go away." Tanner's steady stare made Sophie blush. "God's been working on me. I couldn't see how Burt's idea would work with me in charge. I still can't. But I'll start with your day camp idea and wait for God to lead me from there."

"I hope He comes through for you." How could she have imagined Tanner would be sidetracked by Burt's money? Everything he'd done here was with a view to fulfill Burt's dream.

"God always comes through, Sophie. It's just that sometimes it's in a different way than we expect." He smiled, his straight, even teeth flashing. "At the very least I owe you dinner for helping me get started."

"You don't owe me anything." No way did she want this man to think there would be more than business to their relationship.

"Yeah, I do." His lazy smile was so attractive. "I want to repay you for helping me realize that I don't have to have the whole plan up and running right away. Burt once said it took years for God to get him used to the idea of using Wranglers Ranch for kids. I'll trust God to keep pushing me forward."

"I wish I had your strength," Sophie muttered, not intending him to hear it.

"Lady, you're a lot stronger than I'll ever be." Tanner leaned against the door frame, his hand stuffed into his front pockets. "I could never handle a job, two kids, one of whom I homeschool—"

"Where's Beth?" How could she have gotten so caught up in Tanner that she'd forgotten her daughter? Sophie glanced frantically at the work site where stone masons chiseled a patio.

"I'm here, Mama. I'm coloring." Her daughter sat on the floor in one corner, a book in front of her, crayons neatly organized. "I didn't bother you, Mama. So can we see the bunnies?"

"Sweetheart, you never bother me. And you've been very patient." Sophie hunched down beside her child and pressed a tender kiss against her head. "Just a few minutes more," she promised.

"Okay." Beth happily returned to her crayons.

"She's such a sweet kid," Tanner murmured, his dark green gaze resting on Beth. "It must be great to have a daughter like her. She brims with joy no matter what."

"Yes, she does." Sophie wanted to hug him for saying that. So many people saw only Beth's handicap, yet Tanner— She quashed her admiration for the rancher and returned to the reason she'd come here. "The homeschool group wants to plan an outing to your ranch, if you'll allow them to come."

"Sure." His forehead creased. "When? And what kinds of things will you want to do? I remember you said that not all the kids would be able to ride."

"For this first trip there'll be no riding. Instead we're looking for educational as well as fun." Sophie laid out the board's ideas: a nature walk, a discussion and perhaps a demonstration about a day on the ranch followed by refreshments. "Is that doable?" A leap of pleasure sprang inside at his nod.

"Provided you handle the refreshment part," he said with a grin.

"No problem." A wash of relief filled her at the ease of working with him. "When is a good time for you?"

Tanner consulted the calendar on his phone before giving her a choice of dates. She noted those, promised to get back to him, then glanced around.

"Is something wrong?" he said.

"Just wondering when the patio will be finished." A dozen scenarios for using the area played through her head.

"By the end of tomorrow, I hope. That's what they promised." He smiled at Sophie's surprise. "They'd better finish then because the youth pastor, Mike, is bringing some kids out on Friday evening and he wants them to have a sing-along around a fire."

"So you're already getting kids out here." She grinned at him. "That was fast."

"That was your daughter's doing." He glanced at Beth and chuckled.

"Beth?" Sophie liked Tanner's smile, an open, sharing kind of expression, not the kind of cagey grin that made you worry about what would come next. "What did she do?"

"She spoke to Mike last Sunday. I don't know exactly what she said, but apparently Beth is a great salesgirl. He called me up that night to ask if we could arrange something especially challenging for some tough kids in his group who haven't been engaged by whatever he's been arranging. He's planning a mini rodeo for Friday."

"Can you handle that?" she asked curiously.

"Oh sure." Tanner winked at her. Sophie's stomach dipped. "We'll take out Jezebel, Obadiah and a few other old-timers for the kids to ride. They're gentle and don't spook. We won't be setting any rodeo records but it's all for fun anyway."

"Jezebel and Obadiah, huh?" Sophie couldn't smother her laughter.

"Yep." He grinned at her. "Actually I intended to phone you to see if I could order some snacks," Tanner added. His cheeks turned slightly pink when Sophie checked her watch and then raised her eyebrows.

"Tanner, today is Wednesday. Your event is Friday. I pride myself on freshly made delicious food, but I need time to make it," she scolded. "I have an event on Friday night and another on Saturday."

"I'm sorry. I got caught up in other stuff. Never mind. I'll go to the bakery." He looked so sad about it that Sophie's irritation melted.

"And ruin Wranglers' reputation for the best eats ever?" she teased. "How many kids and what kind of snacks?"

"You'll do it?" Could a grown man's eyes twin-

kle? "The church is supplying hot dogs and fixings. I thought I'd buy some chips so you'd only
need to make treats. For around twenty, Mike
said. I figured a couple pieces for each kid."

"You don't know kids' appetites." Sophie inclined her head. "I'll make lots. If you have leftovers you can freeze them for another time or
take them to church potluck."

"Good idea." His attention strayed to the patio
under construction. "Will the homeschool kids
eat here or would you rather have some kind of
picnic elsewhere on the ranch?"

"The patio would be perfect. A smooth surface makes it a lot easier for kids in wheelchairs."
Sophie knew it was time to leave yet she lingered, savoring the lazy drape of the mesquite
trees where they shaded the corner of the new
patio. Neither the murmur of voices behind her
as deliverymen finished filling the room nor the
construction noise in front detracted from the
peace of this place. "You're so lucky to live here."

"Blessed," Tanner agreed, his voice coming
over her left shoulder. "I thank God every day
that Burt found me and brought me here."

"I never heard the whole story. Will you tell
me?" Sophie asked quietly, intrigued by the
glimpse into Tanner's past.

"Not much to tell. I was almost sixteen, living
on the streets. I'd run away from my foster home."

He grimaced. "I was auditioning for membership in a gang when I met Burt." His cheeks stained red. "Actually I was trying to steal his truck. He invited me out to lunch and I was starving so I went."

"And that's it? You came here?" she asked in disbelief.

"Not quite." Tanner chuckled. "I ate the meal, even had seconds, but when he started talking about God I walked out on him. That didn't stop Burt. He came back, again and again. I must have cost him a fortune in food but the man was relentless."

"So eventually he talked you into coming to Wranglers." Sophie nodded, then stopped at the look on Tanner's face. "Not quite?"

"Not hardly. Burt had done some foster parenting years before so he had connections. He went to a social worker who was a friend of his and reported me." Tanner grinned at her surprise. "She appeared with some cops to take me to a juvenile detention center unless I agreed to have Burt as my guardian. He'd talked a lot about his ranch and since I was keen on horses I agreed to go with him. I figured I'd spend some time at Wranglers, enjoy the food and let my bruises from a street fight heal. Then I'd run away again."

"But you didn't." Sophie's interest grew.

"I didn't have the energy." Tanner shook his

head, his face wry. "That man about wore me out with chores around this place. When he wasn't watching me, Moses was. I almost left the night before I was supposed to go to school, but I couldn't get away from them. Then I realized some of the kids admired me because I lived on a ranch. Me! So I decided to stay for a while."

"And you've never left." Sophie had heard Burt speak about Wranglers Ranch but she'd never realized how much effort he'd put into his work with Tanner.

"God and Burt wouldn't let me." Tanner's face grew pensive. "That man had a faith that astounded me. He prayed about everything and God answered. I couldn't leave because I was desperate to figure out why that was. Because of Burt I finally accepted God in my life. I've never regretted that. God's love changed my world."

Tanner sounded so confident in his faith. Sophie wished she was. But somehow lately she felt out of touch with God, as if He ignored her pleas for a way to build her catering business, to help Davy, to enrich Beth's life. And she still battled to be free of the condemnation her parents had heaped on her head when they'd first learned she was pregnant all those years ago.

*Everybody pays, Sophie. For every action there is an equal and opposite reaction. If you break God's laws, you have to pay the price.*

So now she was a widow, broke and alone with two kids, one mentally challenged and one well on the path to trouble. When would she have paid enough?

"Mama? Can we see the rabbits?"

Sophie shook off the gloomy thoughts to smile at her sweet daughter. Beth wasn't a penalty. She was a blessing. So was Davy.

"Why don't you ask Tanner?" She tossed a glance at the man who was becoming her best customer.

But he couldn't be more than that because Sophie wasn't about to trust Tanner or any other man with more than simple friendship.

When Tanner caught himself straightening a cushion for the fifth time on Friday night, he knew he was fussing too much. Moses knew it, too.

"What's bugging you?" the old man demanded from his seat on the patio. "You're like a cat on a hot roof. Is it that lady?"

"Sophie?" He saw the gleam in the old man's eyes and chided himself for taking Moses's bait. "She said five. She should have been here by now."

"That young pastor is waiting by the front gate for the second bus from the church. Guess I'd better go take the hooligans to the north pasture."

Moses swallowed the last of his water, then rose. "They're playing a game about a flag."

"Capture the flag," Tanner said.

"That's what he called it." Moses nodded and pointed to the dust trail. "That could be your lady."

His *lady*? Tanner didn't have time to sort through the rush of excitement that skittered inside his midsection because Sophie pulled in front of the house and braked hard. She jumped out of her van and hurried to the back.

"Is anything wrong?" He strode toward her, noticing Beth's tear-streaked face in passing. Davy didn't look at him.

"Very wrong," she muttered, handing him two large trays of assorted goodies. Her face was white, her eyes troubled. "But I don't have time to go into it now. I've got to serve crudités at a black-tie event in half an hour."

"The kids?" he asked, balancing the trays in each hand.

"Are staying with me," she said, her voice tight. "They can sit in the corner while I work." Clearly Sophie was steamed.

"Why not leave them with me? They can—" Tanner swallowed the rest of his offer when her dark brown eyes flashed a warning.

Sophie slammed the van's rear door closed,

nodded toward the house and, after ordering the kids to stay put, followed him into the kitchen.

"He stole from you." Her fury showed in her stance, in the flicker at the corner of her mouth and in her lovely pain-filled eyes. "My son stole from you."

"Ah." Tanner clamped his lips closed and said nothing more.

"You knew?" If anything her anger burned hotter. "You knew and didn't say anything?"

"Sophie, he made a mistake. He took the arrowhead without thinking and then he didn't know how to put it back," he said in a soft voice. "But he would have. Davy's not a cheat."

"You could have fooled me." Her shoulders sagged. A rush of compassion filled Tanner. She hadn't even started her job and she was worn out.

"You can't do your best work worrying about them. Leave Beth and Davy here," he insisted softly. "Moses will talk to Davy, and trust me, Moses knows exactly what to say to get your son to consider his actions."

"Reward him by letting him stay?" Her brows drew together.

"Sophie." He watched her watch him. "Davy knows right from wrong. You don't have to bat him over the head with it. What he needs is to see how his actions affect others." He touched her shoulder. "Besides, Beth shouldn't suffer for his mistake. Leave them here. We'll talk later."

She studied him for several minutes, caught sight of the clock and heaved a sigh.

"Are you sure?"

He nodded.

"I don't feel good about this," she said. "I feel like Davy's getting paid for stealing."

"He won't feel like that when he leaves here tonight, I assure you." Tanner squeezed her shoulder. "Go do your job. You can deal with the rest afterward."

"You're always bailing me out," she murmured.

"Seriously?" He waved his hand at the trays of baking. "Who's bailing whom? But let's not argue it. You've got a job waiting and I need to check if Moses needs help. I'll get the kids so you can get on the road."

"You are a very nice man, Tanner Johns." Sophie spared a long moment to study him before she led the way back to her van. "No wonder Burt trusted you." She opened the van door. "Okay, you two, out. You're staying with Tanner till I'm finished with work. And no, this is not a vacation, Davy."

Tanner watched her pin the boy with a severe look that sent him scuttling out of the van. Sophie looked as if she'd say more but Tanner had a feeling Davy needed time to process what he'd done, time away from his mom.

"See you later," he said with a wave, then shepherded the kids toward the house.

Sophie drove away.

"Did Mom tell you?" Davy muttered as they walked.

"That you took something that didn't belong to you?" Tanner shook his head. "She didn't have to. Neither did Moses."

"How come?" Davy frowned as he peeked at Tanner through his lashes.

"I saw you take it when Moses showed you the collection."

"But you never said anything," Davy sputtered.

"Why would I want to hurt your mom by telling her you stole from us?" Tanner looked the boy square in the eye and watched him squirm. "Your mom loves you. It must have hurt her a lot to find out what you did."

"Yeah. I didn't think about that." Davy tried to smile when Beth slid her hand into his and hugged him.

"I love you, Davy," she said.

Tanner's heart pinched. What a special child. They both were. He wanted to reassure them they'd be okay but they weren't his to reassure. All he could do was support Sophie.

"Come on. We need to help Moses with a group

that's visiting." He saw Davy lagging back and urged him forward. "What's the matter?"

"I have to apologize to Moses," the boy said, head down. "What I did was wrong. I knew it and I did it anyway. I wish I hadn't."

"That's the first step to learning," Tanner assured him. Sophie might think she had a problem with this kid but from his perspective, Davy seemed a good kid who'd simply given in to an impulse. Her parenting skills were not at fault and he was going to tell her that the next time they got some time alone together.

Tanner had a hunch Sophie might not like the rest of what he was going to tell her, but he'd just had an idea about how he could help her teach Davy about responsibility, an idea that if carried out, was going to mean he'd have a lot more contact with the single mom.

Now, why did that make him smile?

# Chapter Four

"I can't believe it." A week later Sophie stared at the son she'd struggled to control. "A few hours of after-school work at Wranglers Ranch and Davy seems a different child."

"It's the horses," Tanner said. "Animals who've been abused or mishandled always seem to have a life-changing effect on people who work with them."

"I think it's your effect, too, Tanner." Embarrassed that a stranger could manage her child better than his own mother, Sophie quickly averted her gaze from his intense one.

They stood side by side, silently watching as Davy half carried, half dragged hay to the freshly cleaned stall. The boy glanced once at Tanner, waited for his nod of satisfaction, grinned at Sophie and then continued working, his forehead shiny with perspiration.

"Look at him. I can barely get that same boy to clean his room." She managed a huff of laughter to mask the feeling of failure that bubbled inside.

"Davy's beginning to realize the satisfaction that comes from giving to others." Tanner turned to face her. "Where's Beth today?"

"A friend's birthday party. Believe me, it wasn't an easy choice for her, allotting her favorite cowboy second place to attend a birthday party," she teased.

Tanner shrugged. "Love is fickle."

"You can say that again." Sophie knew he didn't understand how much she meant those words, but since she didn't want to explain and spoil this moment of sharing, she leaned against a fence rail and allowed the dappling sun to warm her. The heat felt good after three hours spent catering in frigid air-conditioning.

"You're tired," Tanner said after studying her. "Do you have time for some tea while Davy finishes his job?"

"That's kind of you." It sounded strange to hear that her son had a job. Sophie debated a moment before she said, "I'd rather have coffee than tea, though."

"You don't want my coffee." Tanner gave a slight shudder.

"I'll make it," she offered, unable to quash her longing for a jolt of caffeine. "It would go well with the leftover cake from my event, if you're interested?"

"Silly question. I'm always interested in cake." Tanner licked his lips before telling Davy to come to the house when he was finished. Then in a much quieter aside he asked his foreman, Lefty, to watch Sophie's son.

"Thank you," she said after she'd retrieved the leftover dessert from her van. "I appreciate your thoughtfulness."

"More like common sense." He held the kitchen door open for her. "We don't leave guests alone with the horses, ever."

"So how is the guest thing coming?" After scooping grounds from the tin he handed her, she added ice water from the fridge and turned the coffee machine on. "Anything new?"

The freshly brewing aroma wafting through the kitchen teased Sophie's nostrils. Apparently it had the same effect on Tanner because he closed his eyes, inhaled and smiled, his mouth stretching wide. Her insides quivered at the attractive picture he made.

"How come I use the same machine, the same coffee, and I never get this aroma?" he demanded when he finally opened his eyes.

"Don't know," she said with a shrug. He grimaced.

"Okay, keep your secrets. Guests?" He nodded,

green eyes intense. "We're getting some calls. Not the street kids I was aiming for, but kids. We have four groups booked for next week."

"Our homeschoolers come on Monday so— three groups besides them? That's good. Isn't it?" Sophie didn't understand why he wasn't smiling. As soon as the coffee finished brewing she poured out two large mugs, opened the cake box in front of him and sat down.

Once he'd fetched cream for his coffee, Tanner sat opposite her. With delicate precision he selected the largest piece of cake, laid it on a plate, then slowly sampled it.

"Is it okay?" she asked, worried by his silence.

"I guess it'll do." He winked as he took a second helping. "Can you make this again next week?"

"I could." She smiled. That wink got to her. Made her feel skittish. Nervous. *Young.* "Things must be improving if you're feeding a group."

"Not for a group. I want to take it to church for potluck Sunday." Tanner licked the icing off his fingers.

"Better not. Everyone at church knows this recipe is mine. I've taken it several times." She chuckled at his glower. "I could make you something else, though."

"Hard to beat this chocolate." He eyed the two remaining pieces but left them.

"Had enough?" Sophie couldn't hide her surprise.

"No way. But Davy will want some." He savored his coffee. "About the groups—I'm getting interest from several different organizations, but I'm hesitant to accept many bookings until we've had your group through and figured out what to expect. I've considered many scenarios but reality is far different from imagining."

"You've checked into insurance and all that?" Funny, Sophie mused to herself. She didn't feel the usual anxiety she experienced when her children weren't under her direct control.

Because she trusted Tanner? No! She couldn't afford to trust anyone.

"What if someone falls or a horse bolts or—"

"Our lawyer says we're covered, Sophie. Not that our horses bolt." Tanner tossed her an abstracted smile, but his forehead furrowed.

"But you're still worried. Why?" Sophie felt his intense scrutiny before he spoke.

"What if that's all we become, Sophie, a kind of entertainment for locals?" His hesitant voice dropped. "Burt's goal was so much bigger than that. The day he found me—" He stopped.

"Doing some initiation for a gang, wasn't it?" She was eager to hear the story behind the story so she asked, "How did you get involved in a gang?"

"I'd been living on the street." He shrugged.

"I was a lifer." When she frowned he explained. "Lifelong foster child."

"You never knew your mother?" Sophie saw sadness fill his face.

"As I understand it, she gave me away right after I was born." A twinge of hurt edged Tanner's husky tone. His chin jutted out defensively. This insecure man was far different from the competent-cowboy image she usually saw.

"Oh, Tanner." She couldn't help reaching out to touch his arm and press her fingers against his warm skin. "I'm so sorry."

"I found out when I was seven. I didn't really understand it then but it didn't take long to figure out that nobody really wanted me, not the way other kids' mothers wanted them." He tried to smile but there was no humor in his next words. "I never stayed in a house more than six months before I was moved. The last one was abusive but the social worker didn't believe me so I ran away."

"And lived on the streets in Tucson," she added.

"Yeah." He nodded. "It was a lot safer than that home." He drained his cup and rose to fetch the coffeepot. When Sophie declined his offer he refilled his own cup. "But I wouldn't do drugs and that put me up against a guy who did."

"You got into a fight and Burt rescued you," Sophie finished.

"Burt sure blabbed." Tanner smiled. "Street

life was tough but it wasn't all bad. I made some good friends. It was just that when they got high they turned into different people." He shrugged. "Anyway I came to Wranglers and stayed."

Sophie knew there was a lot more to the story, things he hadn't said. She wondered what they were but before she could question him further, he turned the tables.

"What about you?" Tanner said. "Why haven't you married again?"

"I don't think I'm the type to be married." Sophie strove to make her response sound carefree, airy. "Anyway I have to focus on my kids."

"And when they're grown?" Tanner arched one brow in a question.

"That'll be ages. Beth will probably be with me for a long while." Sophie couldn't think of anything else to add without going into detail, which she did not want to do.

Fortunately Davy appeared. He gobbled down the cake and a tall glass of water and filled the gaps between with nonstop enthusiasm about his work.

"I want to hear all about it, son," Sophie said half an hour later, delighted by the excitement she heard in his voice. "But you'll have to tell me the rest on the way home. We need to pick up Beth in twenty minutes."

"Aw, Mom—" The words died midsentence

when Tanner cleared his throat. Davy wiped his face on his napkin, rose and stored his dishes in the dishwasher. "I'm ready when you are," he said moments later.

"Great." Blinking her surprise, Sophie glanced at Tanner, who was nodding approvingly at her son. "Could you bring that empty cake box, please?"

Davy instantly obeyed, then stopped in front of Tanner. "Tomorrow's Saturday. Will I be needed for work then?" he asked, his tone quiet and respectful.

"Yes. If your mom can bring you out." Tanner glanced at her, waited for her agreement.

"Bringing him here isn't a problem," she agreed as they walked to her van. "But I'm not sure about picking him up. I'm catering an anniversary tea tomorrow afternoon and I don't know how long I'll be."

"Why don't you come when you're finished?" Tanner invited. "We can share a pizza."

Something about the way he said that sent a frisson of worry tiptoeing up Sophie's spine, sending her independence surging. A pizza might be the first step toward getting involved in a date-type of situation, and she did not want that. She rapidly postulated excuses to refuse, discarding all of them.

"You don't like pizza?" Tanner asked with a frown.

"Yes, I do, but I'm not sure that will work," she said finally.

"Aw, Mom." This time Davy didn't even glance at Tanner, his disappointment in her obvious. "We never do anything special after you finish work."

"It so happens I'd planned pizza and games for tomorrow night," she said quickly. Too quickly.

"Great! Can Tanner come, too?" Davy's brown eyes glowed with excitement.

What could she do but graciously agree? After all, the man had singlehandedly managed to get her son started down a different path. Pizza was the least she owed him.

"Of course you are welcome to join us, Tanner." She hoped her genial tone masked her uncertainty.

"I don't think so." He smiled at Davy to soften his refusal before his gaze returned to Sophie. "Thanks anyway, but you'll be tired after working. Anyway I get the feeling Saturday nights when you're not working are family nights. I don't want to intrude."

"You won't be," Davy insisted. "We need four people to play the games. Otherwise Mom has to play two spots and that takes too long. We need Tanner, don't we, Mom?"

Need him? No, she didn't *need* him. And even

if she did she couldn't afford to need anyone. Still, Davy's plea and the obvious pleasure he found in the cowboy's company was her undoing. Besides, if Tanner came, her son wouldn't nag to go out with his "gang."

"Please join us, Tanner." Sophie swallowed all her inhibitions and smiled. "I'm not Italian but I make a decent pizza."

"With onions?" Tanner kept a straight face when Davy choked off a complaint. "And anchovies?" A burst of laughter exploded from his chest when Davy couldn't control his horrified expression.

"I'm afraid the best I can do is cheese, ham and pineapple, maybe some pepperoni." Sophie mentally checked her store of groceries. She had paid for the ingredients for today's job and tomorrow's tea, which meant her cash was low. There was always her credit card but Sophie hated using that. After Marty died she'd been mired in debt once, and now that she was free she was never going the credit route again.

"A Hawaiian pizza sounds fantastic." Tanner smiled at her. "Thanks. I'd like to come if you're sure I won't be in the way."

"You won't." Davy was all smiles as he climbed into the van. "And you can bring me home so Mom won't have to come get me," he added, his eyes shining with excitement.

"Would that work?" Sophie felt self-conscious as she climbed into her van with Tanner watching.

"Sure. What can I bring? Doughnuts?" He winked at her startled look. "Kidding. Maybe some soda. Or ice cream?"

"You don't have to bring anything," Sophie said. "Just yourself. I've really got to go now. Beth will be waiting. See you."

"Yes, you will, Sophie." Tanner's low words sounded like a promise and that produced a warm glow inside that grew when he smiled at her. "See you tomorrow morning, Davy."

Sophie drove away while ordering herself not to glance in the rearview mirror. But she couldn't help it. She gulped at the sight of Tanner standing there, watching them leave, hat tipped back on his head, hands thrust in his pockets, calm, in control.

What she wouldn't give to feel like she was in control of her world.

"It's great that Tanner can come tomorrow night, isn't it, Mom?" Davy said. "You better make a lot of pizza and something nice for dessert."

"Why?" she asked curiously.

"'Cause Tanner always seems hungry. When I got some water out of the fridge today all I saw was an apple and some juice." Davy went silent for a moment, forehead furrowed as he thought. "Maybe when I go tomorrow I should take some extra sandwiches so I can share my lunch with Tanner."

Sophie sighed. Another mouth to feed. And yet she couldn't smother the smile that lifted her lips. Tanner was so appreciative of whatever she made. It was a pleasure to cook for him.

*Watch it! It's just a plain little family dinner, for the kids' sake. You don't want more than that, remember?*

No, she didn't. But it *was* nice to have her cooking appreciated.

Did that explain the kind of fuzzy afterglow that lingered for hours after Sophie had left Wranglers Ranch?

Tanner walked into the grocery store with purpose. Only he wasn't exactly sure what that purpose was. What did one take for pizza dinner with a gorgeous woman and two kids?

He should have brought Davy with him instead of dropping him at home to clean up. Now he pushed his cart up and down the aisles, puzzling over choices.

Garlic bread? Nah, Sophie probably made her own. Soda? She probably didn't like to give her kids so much sugar. Milk. That was an okay choice, surely? He chose two gallon jugs, then added a couple of pounds of butter. Everyone used butter, didn't they?

Tanner made several trips around the produce section before he came to a decision. Fruit was good for kids. He grabbed a big watermelon, two bags of grapes and three packs of strawberries. He thought only a moment before adding a pail of ice cream. Maybe Sophie would use it for one of her yummy desserts.

Stuff for a salad seemed a healthy idea, so Tanner added fresh vegetables. Sliced salami beckoned and he paired it with a package of sliced ham, just in case she didn't have enough meat to put on the pizza. He selected the largest onion he could find just to tease Davy, then added his crowning achievement—three pounds of freshly ground coffee.

*Please, Lord, let her make that fantastic coffee again*, Tanner prayed silently. He had to go back to get some cream, stomach growling at the thought of homemade pizza and Sophie's delicious coffee laced with cream. It was going to be a good evening.

Unable to think of anything else, he walked to the checkout.

"Stocking up, huh?" The clerk raised her eyebrows as she checked him out. "No doughnuts today?"

"Nope." Tanner almost burst out laughing at

her surprise. "But I will take this." *This* was a pack of candy bars, Davy's favorites. The boy had enthused over them for twenty minutes yesterday. "These mints." For Beth. "And this."

There wasn't anything wrong with taking some flowers to his hostess, was there?

Tanner loaded the bags in his truck while noting the presence of the homeless man in the same place he'd seen him last time. He thought for a moment, returned to the store and purchased a container of soup from the snack bar, a thick ham sandwich and a bottle of icy lemonade. He tucked another ten-dollar bill into the sandwich bag before carrying them outside.

"Hi. I just bought my dinner but it seems I've been invited out and won't need it. Interested?" He held out the items and waited until the man stood. "I'm Tanner Johns."

"The doughnut guy." The man nodded. "I'm Tom. Tom Parker." He peeked in the bag. "I'm not a street person."

"Doesn't matter to me, man. It's just—I used to live on the streets and old habits die hard."

"Yes, but—"

"Wasting a fresh meal seems silly if someone else can enjoy it." Tanner somehow felt it was best not to push for answers just yet. "Still got my card?" When Tom nodded, he said, "Call me if you want. The job offer still stands."

"I can't work—" Tom paused. The pain in his eyes made Tanner want to offer a way for him to avoid explaining. "Not yet anyway."

"I'm sorry, Tom. Listen, I want to talk to you but I can't stick around now or I'll be late, and trust me, there's no way I want to make this lady wait." How could he keep this connection going? "Maybe next time you and I meet we could go for coffee at that ice-cream place? I need an excuse to visit there."

After some hesitation Tom nodded. "Sure. Okay. *If* we meet again."

"We will." The two words slipped out.

"How do you know that?" Tom asked curiously.

"Because I believe in God and He works all things together." Tanner grinned. "Be seeing you, Tom." He swung into his truck and headed for Sophie's. "What do You want me to do about him?" he prayed aloud, but for the moment God wasn't explaining. That was okay. Tanner was learning to wait for God's direction, just like Burt had tried to teach him.

It was only as Tanner pulled into the Armstrong driveway that he started wondering if he'd bought too many things. Sophie certainly seemed to think so when he handed her the flowers, then asked Davy and Beth to help him carry the rest inside.

"Thank you but—what is all of this?" Sophie's dark eyes stretched wide as they plunked bag after bag on the counter. She looked really pretty in a fitted red shirt, cheeks flushed from the warmth of the kitchen, long legs covered in shabby jeans and bare feet.

"I wanted to bring a couple of things, you know, my share of the meal." Tanner inhaled the mouthwatering scent of a robust tomato sauce, spices and freshly baking dough.

"Uh—" Sophie cleared her throat. "A couple of things?" She waved a hand at the stockpile. "You must be planning to eat a lot."

Heat singed his cheeks as he muttered sheepishly, "Maybe I got carried away."

"You think?" She arched one perfectly shaped eyebrow. Tanner had a hunch Sophie would have liked to send some of the bags home with him, but she couldn't because the kids were enthusing over the grapes as if they were some kind of delicacy.

"Thank you for the mints, Mr. Cowboy," Beth said, her sweet smile lighting up her face. "And for everything. Mama said we wouldn't have milk for a while. I love milk."

"Oh. Good. Drink all you like." Tanner smiled to hide his concern. Wouldn't have milk? What did that mean?

"You can have milk with your pizza, Beth."

Sophie's voice came out choked. She coughed, regrouped and thanked him again. "You certainly didn't have to go to all this trouble, though. It's only pizza."

"Homemade pizza," he clarified and winked. "I wanted to make sure I get seconds."

"Seconds and probably thirds." Sophie seemed tense, off-kilter, as if she wasn't sure she wanted him here, in her home. "I have a couple of things to do before it's ready. Would you like to talk to the kids in the other room?"

"I'd like to help, if I can." He waited for instructions but it was clear Sophie preferred to have her kitchen space to herself because she shooed him away. "I'll call when I'm ready," she promised when he hesitated.

"Okay." He followed the kids into the living room and agreed to play a game of checkers.

The coffee table wobbled when he pressed too hard on it and Sophie's couch had some of the same issues Burt's chair had suffered from, so after a few minutes on it Tanner moved to the floor. He saw a number of other problems in the little house that needed addressing—drooping wallpaper, a screen on a window that had come loose and, of course, the stair with the loosened carpet that Davy had tripped over the first time Tanner had visited.

He made a mental note of all of them, though

he figured it would be pretty hard to fix them. Sophie seemed like one of those folks who had a lot of pride and wouldn't welcome his notice of the problems in her home. Still, maybe with Davy's help—

"The pizza's ready if you'd like to come to the table." Sophie glanced at him, something dark and worried lingering at the back of her gaze. Then her smile reappeared as her children hurried to the table. When everyone was seated she glanced at Davy. "Would you please say grace?"

Davy began to protest, then stopped, glanced at Tanner and bowed his head. "Thanks, God, for this good food and for Tanner bringing chocolate bars. In Jesus's name, amen."

"Amen." Tanner stifled his chuckle and watched as Sophie lifted a huge pizza from the oven and set it on the table. His mouth watered just looking at it. He'd never known you could make a pizza look pretty. This one had happy faces all over it.

"Would you like some juice?" Sophie asked, the container of orange juice he'd bought in her hand.

"Just water for me, please. Unless you've made coffee?" She blinked in surprise, then shook her head. "Water is fine. Thank you."

She served him the first piece, the kids next and then herself. Tanner waited until she was seated, amused to notice Davy hurriedly put down his pizza and waited, too.

"Please, go ahead," Sophie said.

Tanner bit into his pizza, unable to speak for the flavors bursting on his tongue. When he asked about them and Sophie explained, Tanner simply listened to her musical voice, knowing he'd never remember what spices she listed. He was too busy enjoying her pretty face. Finally aware that she was watching him with a frown, he savored his pizza and the salad she'd made to go with it.

"I never thought of putting oranges or almonds in a salad but it's delicious," he said. "You have an amazing gift with food, Sophie Armstrong."

"I don't think it's a gift," she demurred, cheeks hot pink. "I just know how to cook."

"That's a gift. A great one." He leaned back in his chair, replete for now. "If you hadn't already done it, I would have suggested you choose cooking as a vocation. Your return rate for customer satisfaction must be amazing."

"I could take on more jobs if I had more time, more equipment and a bigger kitchen," she admitted. She glanced at her children. "Maybe someday I will." When she couldn't coax anyone to eat the last three slices, she lifted the pan off the table. "Ready for dessert?"

"What is it?" Davy asked as Tanner's stomach groaned.

"Banana splits." She set round dishes in front of each of them—not a traditional split but better, much better, Tanner decided as he sampled his portion.

"This is good, Mama." Beth's cheeks were smeared with chocolate sauce but her face glowed with happiness.

"It certainly is, Beth." Tanner frowned. "But you hardly have any, Sophie. Here, take some of mine." He was about to scoop some into her dish when she blocked him.

"This is plenty, thank you." She flushed. "Chocolate heads directly for my hips."

"Does it do that to mine?" Beth twisted to get a better look at her backside.

"Not yet," Sophie assured her, eyes dancing.

Tanner thought her laughter filling the kitchen was the loveliest sound he'd ever heard.

The children finished their dessert, then cleared the table while Sophie made a pot of her delicious coffee.

"I wish I knew how to make this," he said after swallowing his third cup. "There has to be some secret you're not telling me about because the stuff I made this morning, according to your directions, didn't bear the slightest resemblance to this."

"I don't know what to tell you." She studied him for a moment. Tanner felt as if a current ran between them. It gave him an odd feeling, one he'd never had before. He was relieved when she jumped up to wash the dishes. He helped with cleanup, startled by the electricity that sparked when their gazes met or their hands touched. Those sparks were enjoyable.

"Aren't you ever going to be finished?" Davy asked plaintively. "When I do them—"

"Don't go there, son," Tanner warned him with a wink.

"No, because next time it's your turn, Davy." Sophie laughed at his glower. "We're finished." She rinsed out her dishcloth and hung it on the sink, took the last dish from Tanner and set it in the cupboard. "Let the games begin."

Tanner had never played many board games so he lost most of the time, even though Beth tried to help him. Midway through Sophie made popcorn and cocoa and Tanner crunched on the warm buttery corn in between answering questions about the ranch. When he lost all his play money he knew it was time to go.

"I don't know how you won," he said to Beth, chucking her cheek with one finger.

"She always wins," Davy complained.

"It's because Beth is patient. You are too much like me. We want what we want now. Our way."

Sophie's rueful words were accompanied by a wry grimace. "Bethy makes the best of what comes."

"I'll share my money with you, Mr. Cowboy." The little girl shoved a pile of paper money toward him. Tanner's heart melted.

"That's very kind of you, Beth. You keep it safe for us, okay? It's time for me to go home." He rose, hating to leave this family for the loneliness of the ranch house. His gaze rested on Sophie. "Thank you for a wonderful dinner, a delicious dessert and a fun time. I enjoyed myself very much."

"I'm glad." She rose and walked with him to the door, handing him the hat he'd hung on her coat rack. "Come again."

Tanner thought the words were rote, said out of politeness, but he grabbed at them anyway.

"Thank you. I'd like that." He studied her, one arm wrapped around each child. "You're a blessed woman, Sophie. And so are your kids. You have each other and that's a lot." Before he revealed his envy of her, Tanner dragged open the sticky door. Another project. "Good night."

"Good night," they called.

He climbed in his truck, started the engine, but sat there for a moment, watching as the front door closed, the downstairs lights snapped off and the bedroom lights winked on.

What would it be like to have someone like Sophie in your life with a family who was always there for you?

Tanner drove home imagining someone with Sophie's laugh waited for him at Wranglers Ranch.

## Chapter Five

The homeschoolers' visit to Wranglers Ranch was like nothing Sophie expected, mostly because Tanner's efforts outdid her highest hopes for the afternoon.

After a general welcome, he escorted the students on a ramble around the ranch that the children in wheelchairs could easily handle. He paused periodically at stations he'd specifically set up to illustrate different aspects of ranch life.

"Wranglers Ranch is home to a small flock of Navajo-Churro sheep," he explained. The curious children gathered around him, eager to touch the lamb he held before they moved on to examine multicolored balls of wool spilling out of a hand-woven basket. "We sell the wool to artists who use it for their work. On a ranch it's important to have different sources of income."

Sophie's appreciation for the cowboy grew

when, after they arrived at the horse station, he hunkered down to answer the smallest child's query.

"That's a good question," he praised the disabled boy. "We put those hoods on our horses' heads to keep out flies. If we don't, the flies will lay their eggs in the animals' eyes. That would make them really sick and sometimes cause blindness. We want our horses to be healthy."

Tanner's explanation about the brook's importance drew giggles when he said its most important function was to cool off cowboys on hot summer days. He introduced Moses, who delighted the children by escorting them to the remains of an old covered wagon that had once rumbled through Wranglers Ranch. Sophie found herself listening to the man's history lesson as carefully as the children did. Their rapt expressions made their formerly dubious parents smile with approval. Sophie was glad she'd suggested the ranch to the homeschool association. Positive word of mouth from these moms and dads could help Tanner gain new clients.

"Can we come back and ride your horses sometime?" Beth's friend Bertie asked in a loud voice. "I want to ride the white horse and go really fast."

"You'll have to ask your parents about coming back, Bertie." Tanner winked at Sophie. "But maybe you should choose a different horse.

Methuselah doesn't go very fast because he's quite old. Actually he's a grandfather so mostly we let him eat and rest."

"Oh." Quieted for the moment, talkative Bertie fell into step with Beth as Tanner continued the tour. At the completion of it, when the cowboy had finally answered all the kids' questions, their host invited the group to enjoy lemonade and a snack on his new patio.

After ensuring everyone had been served, Sophie turned to find Tanner next to her, offering a glass of lemonade. "Thank you."

"No problem. Thank you for making all these snacks. This should cover it." He held out a check.

"Tanner, I don't expect you to pay for food I made for our homeschool group." Relieved that the parents weren't near enough to overhear, Sophie shook her head in refusal.

"I insist. It's important for Wranglers to track all its expenses. If we know how much our programs cost it will allow us to plan more effectively. Today's visit is a great opportunity to see how our plans worked out."

"But—"

"Also, if future visitors bring food to Wranglers, it will cause a whole mess of issues with the health department." His megawatt grin made Sophie's heart rate soar. "But you're a licensed caterer. Your home-cooked treats make our experience more authentic. Believe me, that's worth paying for."

"Tanner, you've done more than enough by letting us visit," she protested but his smile only grew as he pressed her fingers around the check. He pulled his hand away, then he turned his focus to the trays of treats she'd laid out on a nearby table. After several moments' deliberation he chose a brownie.

"This is amazing," he said after he'd tasted it.

"Personally I like the lemon bars better." Sophie shrugged. "But then I'm not a chocolate addict."

"Like me, you mean?" He chuckled when she wrinkled her nose in dismay at blurting that out. "That's the only kind of addict I don't mind being." Something in the tone of his words made Sophie realize that Tanner's past still troubled him, but she lost that thought when he asked hesitantly, "Do you really think the visit went well?"

"Far better than I ever imagined," she assured him. "Moses was a hit and those stations with your explanations really helped the kids appreciate the past and present at Wranglers."

"The stations were your son's idea." Tanner took another brownie, smiling at her surprise.

"Davy?" She blinked at his nod. "How could he…?" Confused, Sophie waited for an explanation.

"He talked to some of the kids who came here

with the church youth group the other night and realized that many of them had no idea about life on a modern-day ranch." Tanner chuckled at the memory. "Davy confessed he didn't, either, and pointed out that it would be a lot easier for him to help at Wranglers if he understood what we were trying to achieve. So he and I came up with those information stations. He's got a good head on his shoulders, your boy."

"Good to know." Though he'd never said so, Sophie suspected her son longed to earn Tanner's respect. "Davy has changed, thanks to you. I know he has a long way to go to prove himself, but even in the short time he's been coming here, he's grown less self-focused."

"Because he feels needed," Tanner suggested. "Everybody wants to feel like their presence is important to someone, that they have a place. I guess Wranglers is becoming Davy's place."

"I don't think Davy's the only one," Sophie murmured as she glanced around the patio. Parents and children were happily sharing the beautiful space. "This was a good idea."

"You didn't think so at first, though, did you?" His grin dared her to refute it. "When you saw the men putting down the flagstones that day you weren't impressed. But this—" He waved a hand. "This is what I wanted. A space for people to relax, enjoy God's beauty and each other."

"You have a lot of ideas about Wranglers' future, don't you, Tanner?" She knew that she'd underestimated him, hadn't truly considered how he'd use the ranch to minister to kids. "What else would you like to accomplish?"

A strange curiosity welled inside Sophie, a need to share his hopes and dreams. Maybe because it seemed her own dreams would never happen, that she would never escape her desperate scramble to keep a roof over their heads and food on the table.

Tanner didn't have to worry about those mundane things. His dreams could soar. Unlike her he had the means to achieve his goals. And strangely Sophie wanted to be part of that, though she didn't want to get too close to him. Relationships were not part of her life plan.

"I'd like to figure out a way to keep a vet on staff full-time. The county is asking for a medical assessment on each abused horse we take in. It's time-consuming, expensive and hard on the horse to transport, and that's not even mentioning the difficulty of getting in to see a vet in the city. Most don't want to come way out here."

"Great idea," she said. His gaze shifted to something distant, something she couldn't see. "What else?"

"I'd like to build some cabins," Tanner said. "So we could have overnighters."

"Won't that bring additional problems? I mean, sometimes street kids have issues." She frowned, dubious about the idea.

"The whole idea of Burt's camp is to help kids with issues. Everyone has issues, Sophie." He studied her for a moment, then spoke in a quiet, husky tone. "Or maybe I'm just trying to recapture my childhood."

"How so?" Curiosity about his past ballooned.

"When I was ten, I went to summer camp." His voice altered, his joy obvious in his sparkling smile. "It was the one and only time. I've never forgotten the experience because for a while, for one short week, it was okay just to be myself, a kid, and to have fun."

A lump filled Sophie's throat.

"Six of us stayed in a ramshackle leaky cabin with a counselor. It was a dump but I thought it was paradise. I could let myself sleep at night because the counselor was there protecting us." A quirky smile lifted Tanner's lips.

Sophie's heart gave a bump at the sudden rush of attraction that surged inside her. The cut on his cheek she'd seen the day they'd met had almost completely disappeared. She thought perhaps making Burt's dream live was helping Tanner heal in many ways.

"The best part wasn't the sleeping, though," he continued. "The best part came just before sleep. Everyone was in bed. The cabin was dark and quiet. That's when the counselor would talk to us. Not preachy stuff, just telling us we were loved, encouraging us not to ever give up on our dreams. He'd urge us to resist the bad stuff we encountered, make us feel hopeful about our future. It was the first time I can ever remember feeling safe."

He hadn't felt safe until he was ten—almost Davy's age. Sophie's mother's heart ached for that young boy who'd been so alone.

"I've hung on to those moments through some pretty tough times in my life." Tanner smiled at her. "Those feelings—hope and safety—that's what I want Wranglers to give kids. I want this place to show God to kids so they'll yearn to know Him because He's the answer to every seeking heart."

"I think you'll do it, Tanner." How could she not support a dream like his? "There's a lot of space on this ranch and plenty of little groves where cabins wouldn't have to stick out."

"I'm praying for someone, an architect maybe, to show me how to do that, but I need a lot of things in place before building cabins can happen." He shrugged. "Like maybe—clients?"

"They'll come." Somehow Sophie was certain of that. Tanner was the kind of man who reached for his dream and got it. Not the kind of selfish dreams Marty had chased; not for an easy way to make his own world better. Tanner's dreams had a plan and a spiritual grounding. They were for others, not to benefit himself.

Sophie liked the rancher's selflessness. Liked it a lot. Too much for a woman who was never going to let her heart feel anything again.

"Sophie, I really appreciate you doing this on such last-minute notice." Tanner stood in the doorway of Wranglers' kitchen several days later stunned by the number of food trays covering every possible surface. "How did you manage to produce so much so fast?"

"I always keep frozen stock." She looked lovely even with a dab of flour on one cheek.

"Pastor Jeff didn't tell me much, only that something had happened to the couple's venue and they were forced to cancel their wedding," he explained. "Apparently they've waited a long time and desperately want to get married today. Pastor Jeff seemed to think the ranch would be the perfect place for that."

"Didn't they have a caterer lined up?" Sophie swung a tray from one of the ovens and quickly replaced it with another.

"They did. Unfortunately that was canceled with the venue and the chef took another job."

Noticing the line of perspiration dotting Sophie's upper lip, he offered to help.

"That's kind of you but it only looks like chaos." She grinned. "Actually I'm fine and Monica and Tiffany will be here soon to help." She glanced around and nodded, apparently satisfied with her creations. "What about outside?"

"Outside?" Tanner glanced out the window. "What do you mean?"

"Decorations. Something to make it look like a wedding." When he stared at her stupidly, Sophie pointed. "Those bougainvilleas—why don't you drape them to make an arch? It would be the perfect place for the couple to say their vows. There are fairy dusters around the edge of the patio so their colors will really stand out, but maybe you and Davy could snip some brittlebush flowers."

"Moses will put up a fuss if I appropriate your son. Davy's *helping* him with a new horse." Tanner chuckled when she rolled her eyes.

"If we had flowers we could put them in small glasses on each of the table for centerpieces. Beth's gathering petals off those bushes next to the sycamore trees. She loves scattering them." Sophie's brown eyes softened with love. "But something with stems would be nice."

"Centerpieces, huh?" Tanner studied her. "How do you know about this stuff?"

"I was a bride once." Sophie thrust out her

chin. "Not that we had a fancy wedding. My parents weren't anxious for their friends and neighbors to know I had to get married." For a moment she looked grim. Then her irrepressible grin reappeared. "I'm a girl, Tanner. Weddings are in our genes."

"Ah." He felt awkward and ignorant on the subject so he went outside to work on the bougainvilleas as requested. When he stood back to get the full effect, he realized how right Sophie was. The arch made a perfect focal point for a bride and groom.

"Mama said you'd show me what to do with these petals." Beth stood at the edge of the patio, a basket hanging from one hand.

"She did?" Tanner gulped, totally out of his depth. "What do you think we should do with them?"

Beth considered for several moments, then smiled, her blue eyes glowing.

"We can make a little path to that," she said, indicating the arch. "And we could sprinkle some on the tables and benches. They smell nice."

"Can you show me how to do it?" he asked hopefully. Beth did, insisting he handle the petals gently. Ten minutes later his patio looked romantic and sort of dreamy.

"Good job," Sophie approved. She hugged Beth, then addressed him. "Maybe with your pet-

als decorating things we don't need centerpieces."
She turned to Tanner. "If I were you, I'd order
some tablecloths, maybe black, to fit these tables.
Then you'd have something fancy to dress up this
area for other special occasions. Who knows, you
might get other weddings."

"I hope not," Tanner told her, aghast at the
thought.

"Wasn't it you who told the homeschool kids
that a ranch needs many sources of income?"
Sophie shot him an arch look. "Not only could
weddings do that, but it would get you additional
exposure."

Maybe she was right but surely there were
other ways to do that without getting involved
in something as personal as a wedding. Tanner
stuffed down his inhibitions long enough to help
her set up the two portable tables she'd brought.
Then he stood back and watched as she and her
staff, with Beth's help, organized a beverage station around a punch fountain.

"Would you be able to man this?" Sophie faced
him with a speculative look.

Him? Serve punch in those itty-bitty plastic
glasses? Tanner gulped and shook his head. "No."

"Why not?" She frowned. "Change into black
pants and a black shirt, or white, and you'll look
like one of us." When he didn't agree, Sophie
glared at him. "I can't do the food *and* serve

punch *and* watch the hors d'oeuvres. We need your help and there's not much time."

She was doing this to help *him*. Tanner sighed, raced upstairs and took a quick shower before changing into the requested clothes. He added the jacket he'd bought for Burt's funeral, gave his boots a swift shine, then hurried back downstairs. And stopped dead in his tracks. Sophie had wreaked bridal magic in less than ten minutes.

"I hope you don't mind," she said from behind him. "That lace tablecloth was in the drawer. I thought it made a nice background for the signing table. And the candles were just sitting in a cupboard. They were half-used but now that they're lit you don't notice that." The words spilled out, as if she expected him to object.

Did he look that dumb? Tanner wanted to hug her.

"Moses and Davy brought over the wagon wheel and the hay bales," she continued. "And your hands helped us set them up. It'll make a good backdrop for pictures."

She'd even found the old bell Burt had unearthed last year from a nearby abandoned mission. It hung above the arch, grit and grime removed, shining in the sunlight.

"You need to expand your business to wedding planner," he praised. "This is amazing."

"I hope they like it." Sophie's brown gaze gave

him the once-over. "You clean up nice, Mr. Cowboy," she said with a giggle in her voice.

Tanner absorbed the sweet sound of her laughter. No matter how busy, Sophie made every occasion fun. He couldn't have asked for a better partner.

*Partner?* Wait a minute…

"Sounds like the guests are arriving. Can you welcome them and show the way, Tanner?" Sophie called her staff, gave Beth a keep-busy job and hurried to the kitchen. She paused at the door to frown at him. "Tanner?"

"Yeah?" *Partner?* He didn't need, didn't *want* a partner.

"As the host at Wranglers, getting the guests to the patio is your responsibility." Her tone asked why he was still standing there.

"I'm hosting a wedding. Right." Tanner took a deep breath as he absorbed this new role. He walked to the front of the house while ordering his brain off the subject of Sophie Armstrong. She was a friend, a very helpful friend. But that's all she was. All she could be. Because his goal was to make this ranch a haven for kids, not to get sidetracked by a lovely mom.

But why had God sent a wedding his way?

A couple stood beside their car, clearly wondering where to go, so Tanner squared his shoulders and stepped forward. He could do host as well as the next guy—he hoped.

"Hello. Welcome to Wranglers Ranch. Are you here for the wedding? Come this way, please."

Twenty minutes later when the patio was almost filled with guests, an old Chevy, fully restored, pulled up. A senior man in a black suit escorted an older woman in a pretty cream silk outfit from the car. Arm in arm, they walked slowly toward Tanner, the woman evidently needing the man's support.

"Hi. We're the bride and groom. I'm Herb Jenkins and this is my bride, Vanessa." Herb thrust out his hand and Tanner shook it.

"Congratulations," he said, suddenly aware that Sophie was beside him.

"I'm Sophie. We thought you might like a bouquet." She handed Vanessa a bunch of multicolored roses he recognized as coming from a shrub out back. "Our friend Moses picked them for you and wrapped them in his handkerchief. Something borrowed."

"Oh, thank you, dear." Vanessa clutched the little bouquet as if it were from a renowned florist. "It's lovely. Now all I need is something blue."

"I have a blue ribbon." Beth squeezed in beside her mother. "You can borrow it," she offered with her sweet smile as she slid a bow from her hair.

"Thank you, darling. You are all so kind." Vanessa sniffed as Beth tied the blue ribbon around her flowers. The groom chuckled as he dabbed at his bride's cheeks.

"Now, Van, don't start crying or we'll never get down the aisle." He looked at Tanner. "Where is the aisle?"

"The patio is this way. Please, follow me." Sophie and Beth slipped through a hedge near the kitchen as Tanner led the couple on a route that emerged at the rear of the patio behind their guests. "Pastor Jeff is waiting for you up there," he said to the groom, who smiled fondly at his wife-to-be, let go of her hand and strode eagerly forward.

"Thank you for doing this on such short notice," Vanessa said. "We've waited for this day since I was diagnosed with breast cancer a year ago. Herb stayed right by my side the whole time while the Lord came through for us. And He's done it again. This is a beautiful place."

"I wish you the very best in your marriage." Tanner glanced around. "Are we waiting for someone to walk you down the aisle?"

"No." Her face saddened. "Our children don't approve. Would you—no, never mind." Her hopeful look died. Tanner couldn't stand it.

"I'd be honored to walk you down the aisle, ma'am."

"You're so kind." She touched his cheek.

"Would it be too much to ask the little blonde girl to be my flower girl?"

"I'm sure Beth would love that." Tanner hurried away to have a quick word with Sophie, then returned with Beth. "Here we are. Vanessa, this is Beth."

"Hi, Beth. Thank you for being part of our wedding." Vanessa touched her cheek, her eyes misty. "You remind me of my daughter when she was your age."

Afraid the bride would start crying, Tanner cleared his throat.

"You know what to do?" he asked Beth, who calmly nodded. As if this was a normal day in her life, she took her place in front of the bride, waiting. "Okay. So whenever you're ready, Vanessa." He held out his arm for her to slip her hand through.

"I've been ready to be married to Herb for such a long time." Eyes riveted to her smiling groom, Vanessa took his arm, then glided over the flagstones as if they were glass. "Hi, Herb," she breathed as if she hadn't seen him for days.

"Sweetheart, you are so beautiful."

Tanner's heart thudded at the love flowing between the couple. He'd never quite believed such love existed until today, but it was clear that these two belonged with each other. Though Tanner had never been in a wedding party before, he suddenly knew exactly what to do. He lifted Vanessa's hand from his arm and tucked it into Herb's.

"Be happy," he said, then, grasping Beth's hand, he stepped aside. They slipped out of the way between two shrubs so the guests' view of the couple wasn't blocked. He followed Beth, who headed for Sophie, who stood near the open doors of the house watching as Pastor Jeff greeted the guests and then addressed the couple.

"Herb and Vanessa, you have already loved each other through better and worse, through sickness and health. You know that love isn't about finding the right person, it's about being the right person, one who stands firm against life's storms but can also give way when needed. One who helps you be the person God created." The pastor's fondness for the couple laced his words. "I'm very proud today to lead you through your vows to each other."

They were the kind of old-fashioned vows that were heartfelt, filled with promise. The kind that said, "I'm sticking with you forever." The kind Tanner had once longed to hear.

*What woman would say those vows to you if she knew you abandoned your own child?*

"I now pronounce you husband and wife. You may kiss your bride."

Wondering if the ceremony brought back painful memories for Sophie, Tanner glanced at her and was startled to find her dark eyes fixed on him, something he couldn't understand swirling in their depths.

"Vanessa and Herb invite you to sample the punch and hors d'oeuvres while they sign the papers," Pastor Jeff said, breaking the spell that held them.

"Okay, we're on," Sophie whispered. "You're pouring the punch, Tanner." She nudged his arm to jolt him out of his fugue.

"Right." He straightened and thrust away his dreams of getting married, having a family. Hadn't he learned that wasn't for him? Instead God had given him Wranglers and a camp to run.

"If you need anything, motion to the girls or me but stay at your station. Okay?" Once he nodded, Sophie hurried away to check the trays her helpers were holding, ready to mingle among the group.

Tanner should have been nervous. Hosting a wedding was something he knew less than nothing about. But he had only to glance at Sophie to know that everything was going perfectly. Classical music played in the background—who'd thought of that?—and a low hum of conversation carried on the gentle breeze as Sophie's staff circulated among guests. Tanner kept pouring until he was sure everyone had a glass of punch to join in the pastor's toast to the happy couple. Gentle laughter filled the air as everyone cheered.

The guests mingled, sometimes sitting at the tables, moving, eager to sample the changing variety of food that Sophie offered as they laughed and shared stories about the couple. Tanner snitched several samples and found it delicious. How had Sophie managed to create a feast in such a short time?

"Tanner, can you help me, please?"

He hadn't seen Sophie come up behind him. Swallowing the last bite of food, he dabbed his mouth on a napkin. "What do you need?"

"Help to move the wedding cake," she whispered. "I thought we could use the signing table and set the cake on that."

He was game to help until he saw the cake. Trepidation made him freeze.

"What's wrong?" Sophie hissed.

"What if I drop it?" He flinched at the glare she threw his way.

"Don't" was her gritted response.

Heart in his mouth, Tanner held the board on one side of the two-tiered cake and gingerly moved it with her out the door and across the patio under Beth's soft directions.

"Good girl, Beth," Sophie said, her voice tender. "Just stay there, okay?"

"Okay, Mama." Beth smiled her unconcerned

smile, trust in her mother complete. Tanner wished he'd known that kind of trust for his own mother. He wished he could instill that kind of trust in his own family. That wasn't going to happen.

"Can I set it down now? Please?" he begged, heaving a sigh of relief when she nodded, glad the cake finally rested on the table. "When did you get a wedding cake, Sophie?"

"I baked it after you phoned me about the wedding last night. I hope it's okay." She arranged some sugar roses in soft pastel hues on the top, added some pale colored sprinkles and a gathered-fabric thing around the base.

"But I phoned after eleven o'clock last night," he gasped. How did she manage to look so rested creating so much? "It looks amazing," Tanner complimented when she stood back to survey her work.

"Thank you." She motioned to one of her helpers to bring plates and pulled a cake server out of her pocket. Once everything was arranged, she stood back for one more look and nodded her satisfaction. "I sent Davy to tell Moses to get some pictures of this. Tanner, you can tell our couple they can cut the cake whenever they're ready."

"Me?" he protested but Sophie had disappeared inside the house. He sent a quick prayer that she was making coffee, then did as he was told.

"A wedding cake? We never expected that." Vanessa's glow brightened to an even higher wattage. "You've made this a wonderful day. A perfect day."

"I'm glad." And he was, Tanner realized. Not that he'd done much. It was all Sophie. She was an amazing woman.

"Cake cutting," Pastor Jeff announced.

Tanner moved away as the group crowded around the couple to watch with Moses snapping madly. When the cake was cut, Tanner felt vaguely disappointed to see Sophie had made them a lemon wedding cake. He'd hoped for chocolate. Which was silly. This would be as delicious as everything else she made.

When he saw her struggling to carry a big urn across the patio, Tanner hurried to help. Her assistants set out cups and spoons along with cream and sugar and two massive teapots. When all was ready for the guests, Tanner followed Sophie to the kitchen, carrying two cups of steaming coffee.

"Sit down and relax," he ordered as he placed one in front of her. "Celebrate another of your successes."

"I hope everything was okay." She sipped her coffee. After a huge sigh she leaned back in her chair. "That was a rush."

"Do you think there will be any cake left?"

Tanner asked, noticing that Beth had a piece and was eating it.

Sophie burst out laughing after she stopped Beth from offering hers.

"What's so funny?" he asked with a frown.

"I made Beth her own cake. I made you one, too." She laughed when he licked his lips. "Well, you'll have to share with Davy and Moses, but mostly your own."

"Where is Davy?" He eagerly accepted the plate of cake she handed him. Lemon cake was light-years better than no cake. "I haven't seen him for ages."

"He and Moses are up to something, a surprise, Moses said. Should I be worried?" Sophie didn't look worried. She looked happy, relaxed, satisfied.

"With Moses? Probably. This cake is amazing." Tanner debated hiding the rest for later, then decided Moses would find it anyway. He'd have to share. "So is the coffee. Your mama is an excellent cook," he said to Beth. "She's giving Wranglers quite a reputation."

"Is that good?" Beth paused, her forkful of cake hanging in midair as she studied him.

"It's very good," he assured her.

"I think so, too." She calmly resumed eating her cake.

"You're a very smart girl, Beth." Tanner smiled

at her, loving the way her blue eyes glowed at the compliment.

"I am? Why?"

"Because you don't worry about things. You trust." Tanner figured there was a lesson there for him.

"Don't you?" The little girl frowned. "In the Bible God says to cast your cares on Him. Right, Mama?"

"Right." Sophie leaned over to nudge Tanner's shoulder with her own. "It's her favorite verse so don't argue."

"Wouldn't dream of it." Her tone spoke of her pride in her child. What a great mom she was, Tanner thought.

"But that's not all of the verse, Mr. Cowboy." Beth studied him with an intensity that made him sit up straight. "Do you know why we cast our cares on Him?" Her blue gaze demanded an answer.

"Uh, no." A six-year-old girl was teaching him the Bible. "Tell me why, Beth."

"Because He cares for us." Her smile spread from cheek to cheek.

He'd never heard the truth of God's love given so succinctly with such passion.

"As I said, you're a very smart girl." Tanner brushed her cheek with his knuckles in a fond caress while his heart yearned for a child like Beth to love.

*You turned your back on that opportunity.*

All Tanner could do now was enjoy Sophie and her kids and pour his heart's desire to be part of something bigger than himself into Wranglers Ranch.

And pray that would be enough to satisfy the ache to be loved that had been throbbing inside him for years.

# Chapter Six

"My mom wasn't too impressed with me and Moses tying those cans on the bride and groom's car," Davy told Tanner a few days after the wedding.

Because neither of them could see her sitting behind her house, Sophie grinned. Truthfully she'd been amused by the action, but that had been tempered by worries about the bridal couple's reaction when they saw the crude cardboard sign proclaiming Just Married. Thankfully Vanessa and Herb had hooted with laughter, so Sophie had tempered her scolding of Davy for touching other people's property, especially after Moses insisted the idea was his.

"I like doing things with you, Tanner. You make everything fun." There was Davy's hero worship showing again. In fact both her kids adored the big rancher, and Sophie had to admit she wasn't immune to his charms, either. The thing was, though catering at Wranglers Ranch was fun, she couldn't depend on it. She could depend only on herself.

"I like doing things with you, too, Davy." Tanner paused, a hesitancy in his voice that tweaked Sophie's attention so that she focused on his next words. "I never knew my parents. Sometimes when I'm with you, I think about them and all the things we could have done together."

"I heard about people finding their real parents. Couldn't you do that?" Davy asked.

"My mom gave me away when I was born. I don't think she'd want me to find her." Tanner sounded definite.

"That must make you sad." Sophie wanted to cheer for Davy's sensitivity.

"Sometimes." Tanner cleared his throat. "I'm glad you're out of school today. I'm hoping your mom won't mind if you and Beth come out to Wranglers. I need some help with an idea I have, kid kind of help."

Sophie could almost see the grin on Tanner's face. She knew his eyes would be dancing with fun. And for some odd reason that made her stomach skip.

*Get a grip, Sophie.*

"Your mom is welcome to come, too, if she wants," Tanner added.

Like she was an afterthought. Sophie's smile faded.

"I'll ask her. Mo-o-o-m!" Davy's bellow echoed through the house.

"She's cutting the rosebushes," Beth called back.

Sophie jumped from her lawn chair, grabbed her pruning shears and barely made it to the bush before Davy and Tanner appeared in the backyard. "Hi," she said to Tanner. "Davy, don't yell, please."

"Tanner wants me and Beth to go to Wranglers," Davy said.

Sophie looked at Tanner curiously. "To do what?"

"If you want to come along, I'd rather show you." He glanced at her rosebush. One eyebrow lifted. "You don't seem to be making much progress. You could do this later."

"I don't know if I can do it at all," she admitted self-consciously. "I'm not good with roses. Apparently I cut off too much last year but the book says they need to be pruned so…" A funny expression washed over his face so she stopped talking.

"I don't think what you're doing is *technically* called pruning," he said, a muscle flicking at the corner of his lips as if he was trying not to smile. "Butchering, maybe. May I?" He held out his hand for her shears.

"Go for it." When she handed them over, he gripped them, studied the shrub for a few moments, then began deftly clipping away branches. A second later droplets of blood dotted his hands where the thorns had pierced.

"You should have gloves on, Tanner." Sophie peeled off her own and held them out. "Those barbs can cause a lot of damage."

"To you maybe. I have tough skin." He ignored her gloves, swiped away the blood and continued working. A few minutes later he leaned back to admire his work. "There. If you leave it alone it should soon start to bloom."

"That'd be the first time since my dad bought it," Davy mumbled after a sideways peek at Sophie.

"Thanks for that, Davy." She gave him a pseudofierce look, took the shears from Tanner's outstretched hand and stored both in her tiny work shed. When she turned around, Tanner had carried the thorny stems to the trash container at the back of her yard. "Thank you."

"You're welcome. So can you come to Wranglers?" He sounded eager for her acceptance. Sophie's heart gave a little skip, which she ruthlessly suppressed. "You don't have to cater today, do you? Not on Martin Luther King Day."

"I don't have *catering* scheduled, no." She wanted to go with him, wanted desperately to escape the thousand repair jobs that never seemed to get done and have fun. But being the one in charge meant facing responsibility. "However, I do have a long list of things that need doing. I want to finish them today."

"Okay. We'll help." Tanner's eyes, dark emerald with swirls of turquoise, danced with fun. "With Davy and Beth and me pitching in, your list will soon be done and then we can all go. What's first?"

"But—" Sophie hadn't expected this. "I—er, that is, I don't know if you can help." She so did not want him to examine the inadequacies of where she lived. Maybe he'd think she wasn't a good mother for raising her kids in such a tumbledown place.

"Try me." When Sophie didn't respond Tanner turned to Davy. "What's first on the list?"

"Fixing that stupid carpet on the stairs." Davy's sour look said it all. "Every time I come down those stairs I trip."

"Carpet repair it is. Do you have a hammer and some small nails?" Tanner asked Sophie.

She hesitated but there was no point. She knew from his face that he wouldn't give in. He'd made up his mind and he was going to help her, whether she liked it or not. And actually, Sophie liked it.

"Thank you. That's very kind of you." She smiled at him, secretly hoping Tanner would also notice the loose board on the downstairs landing. She'd caught her toe on it last night and it still throbbed. "Davy can show you where the stuff is in the shed. I'll get Beth started on cleaning the cupboards."

Once she'd demonstrated to Beth how to clean one cabinet, Sophie got to work washing windows. Inside was simple, but the outside glass required a ladder. She was struggling to move it out of the shed when it was lifted from her hands.

"What's this for?" Tanner asked. "And where do you want it?"

"I'm cleaning windows. I'll start at the back." She thanked him when he'd placed the ladder and was about to climb up with her bucket and cloths when Beth called for her help. "I'll be right back," she promised.

Once Beth was settled, Sophie returned outside. To her surprise Tanner and the ladder were missing. She walked around the side of the house and found him polishing the big picture window at the front.

"Two more on the side and this job can be crossed off." Tanner's wide grin stretched across his face. "Many hands make light work," he said, inclining his head toward Davy, who was washing a basement window.

Funny how the more she got to know Tanner, the less she noticed his faults—if he had any. Sophie had often wondered if she found fault in men because it gave her a good reason to avoid connections with them. But with Tanner...

"What should I do when I'm finished here?" he asked, scrubbing vigorously.

Sophie had dearly hoped to clean up the pile of debris outside her back gate. But she certainly wasn't going to ask Tanner to pick through her garbage. Without answering she hurried inside to answer Beth's call. By the time she returned outside Tanner was storing the ladder in the shed.

"Was painting the fence on your list?" Tanner inclined his head toward the paint cans sitting on a shelf.

"I asked the man I rent from to have the fence painted but he refused. So I told him I'd do it if he'd buy the paint." Sophie felt foolish when Tanner's lips tightened. "I thought if I did some home improvement that he didn't have to pay for, he wouldn't raise my rent."

"Painting is something I could show Davy how to do," Tanner said quietly, his gaze tracking Davy as he picked up debris around the yard. "He wants to feel like the man of the house."

"I know," she murmured, glad when Davy disappeared to discard his trash and couldn't overhear. "I am trying to teach him responsibility but I don't want to put too much on him yet. He's still just a little kid."

"Sophie, Davy is very bright. I think a task like painting would make him feel like he has an important part in the good of his family," Tanner insisted in a quiet tone. "Besides, a newly painted fence is something he could show off to his friends."

"True." How did a single rancher know so much about kids? "But it's a lot of work for you. And he'll make a mess."

"So? What's a mess when you're building character? Burt taught me that." He waited, watching her. "Should we do it?"

"Are you sure you want to?" Sophie asked, dubious about letting Tanner help so much.

Tanner grinned but didn't answer. A moment later he carried the paint cans outside and Davy brought the paintbrushes. He and Davy stashed the debris by the gate in trash bags, then Tanner began showing her excited son how to load his brush and reach the nooks and crannies.

"We'll do this right, Mom," Davy promised in a proud voice. "You don't have to watch us." Tanner winked and made a shooing motion, eyes glinting with fun.

"Thank you, gentlemen." Sophie hurried inside, where she could give her laughter free rein. Might as well admit she liked the owner of Wranglers, liked him a lot. It was good to have a friend who so generously lent a hand.

As long as she didn't let it become more than friendship.

"Mama? I'm finished. Can I paint with Davy?"

Uh-oh. Beth's expectant blue eyes begged her. But Sophie wasn't going to saddle Tanner with another child. Not yet anyway.

"You can," she agreed. "Only we're not going to paint the fence. We're going to paint that cupboard I bought at the garage sale. What color do you think it should be?"

"Blue," Beth said predictably. "I like blue."

"I know you do." Sophie risked a quick glance out the window and did a double take. Tanner was making swift progress. "How about if we paint the cupboard white and then add some blue flowers?"

"I like blue flowers." Beth nodded with a sweet biddable smile.

"I love you, Beth." Swallowing a rush of emotion, Sophie wrapped her sweet daughter in a hug. "You're my blessing."

"Count your blessings," Beth sang in an off-key tone as she nestled against her mother for a moment, then drew back. "Can we paint now?"

Chuckling, Sophie went to find a drop cloth,

paint and brushes. Maybe Tanner's appearance outside the grocery store that day had been an answer to prayer for her little family. It certainly had been for those rabbits! But Sophie wasn't ready to entirely trust God with her future because relying on someone other than yourself always led to hurt when the person disappointed you.

In her adult faith journey, Sophie had endured a bellyful of disillusionment. All through her marriage she'd known she wasn't a good wife. She'd repeatedly begged God to show her how to love Marty as a wife should in spite of the financial predicaments he kept putting them in.

She'd pleaded for His help every time her husband blew their tiny savings and waited interminably for God to respond. His lack of response had left her scrambling to survive after Marty's death. Those desperate days had made Sophie determined she would never be that vulnerable again, never again be totally dependent on anyone but herself.

Like God, Tanner was great to have around. But also like God, he had his own goals, his own desires and his own plans—plans that didn't mesh with hers. One day Tanner wouldn't be part of her world anymore. Sophie needed to keep repeating it to herself. She couldn't let herself rely on him.

That way lay pain and Sophie never wanted to hurt like that again.

\* \* \*

"So my idea is to make a climbing wall here."

After Sophie had checked off all her jobs and couldn't think of another thing, she'd provided a delicious picnic in her backyard. It was such fun that Tanner was loath to break it up, but when they'd eaten and cleaned up, he'd insisted on driving them to Wranglers Ranch.

Now he gave voice to the tumble of ideas that had begun swirling in his head before midnight last night and were still going strong. He felt a surge of relief that Davy and Beth were busy playing with the rabbits because he wanted to hear Sophie's honest perspective.

What he hadn't figured out was why her concerns seemed so important to him.

"A climbing wall? Here?"

The time Tanner had spent with Davy at Sophie's house today had made him aware that not only had he missed special moments like those with his own parents, but also with his own child, the one he'd never known. Suggesting ways Davy could reason with the school bully, empathizing over his fatherless state and explaining why the stars moved in the sky were the kind of things a kid needed a parent for.

Throughout the day Tanner's self-doubts about his decision to never contact his child grew. Davy and Beth's nonstop questions were the very things his own child might ask. Who'd been there to answer them? Who was there now, teaching his son or daughter about God's love? Bad enough Tanner had cheated his child of a father, but was he also cheating his child out of a spiritual relationship with God?

"Tanner?" Sophie's hand on his arm stirred him from his troubling thoughts. "What's wrong?"

"Uh, just thinking," he mumbled, hesitant to share his dark secret past with her.

"About what?" She glanced to check on her children. Then her dark brown stare returned to him, a question in its depths.

Dare he ask her opinion? It took but a moment for Tanner to decide. Sophie was level-headed, totally focused on her kids' welfare. She'd know what he should do.

"A friend broached me with a problem. I'm not sure how to help him. Care to offer an opinion?" he said, deciding he'd frame the situation as hypothetical.

"I don't know that my opinion would count for much," she demurred.

"Oh." Tanner couldn't help it. His face fell, his shoulders sagged. He exhaled.

"But if you want to tell me the issue, I'll tell you what I think, even if it's not what you want to hear," she said with a quick grin.

"Great." How to begin? "This guy…he walked

away from his pregnant girlfriend when he was just a kid—a teenager." Tanner saw her face tighten into a scowl and hurried on. "It was a bad decision. He soon realized that, but when he went back to find her she was gone. He lost all contact. Now he's thinking that he should find his child."

"So why doesn't he?" she demanded, her voice spirited.

"He's worried that doing so might complicate his former girlfriend's life, or the child's. He doesn't want to mess things up for them simply to salve his own guilt, but he does want to know his child. He's always wanted that." As a scowl furrowed her forehead, Tanner began to wish he hadn't said a word. But he could hardly stop now. "You're the kid expert, Sophie. What would you advise him to do?"

"Seriously?" She looked furious. "You're telling me this guy abandoned his pregnant teenage girlfriend—what? Eight or ten years ago?" He nodded. "And you think he should waltz back into their lives now because he has this sudden yen to know his child?" The sarcasm in her voice chewed him out.

Guilt fell like a shroud. But guilt wouldn't help. "It's not sudden. He's wanted—I think he's wanted," Tanner substituted, trying to remember that he was talking about his friend, "—to know his child from the beginning. But he was only sixteen and he was scared and—"

"He was scared. Oh, well, that changes everything," Sophie snapped. "Because she wasn't scared, I guess. She was alone, pregnant, struggling as her body went through changes, giving birth alone, a kid trying to care for her baby on her own, and he was scared. Really?"

Desperate to end her scathing opinion of *his* actions, Tanner went for levity. "So I'll take that as a 'No, you don't think he should find his child'?"

"I think it's too late for his regrets. If he wants to salve his conscience he should write a check." The way she glared at him made him wonder if she'd guessed it was his child they were talking about.

"What if the child needs help?" Tanner sighed. "He made a mistake, Sophie. We all make them, but now he's trying to make amends. You can't just write him off. He's looking for practical advice to do what's best for his child. Shouldn't I suggest he find the mom and the kid and make sure they're okay?"

She frowned at him, her eyes scanning his face. Tanner wondered if he'd pressed her too hard.

"It sounds like this guy must be a really close friend of yours," she said finally. "I'm sorry if I dissed him. It's just—I have no patience with people who opt out when the going gets tough. Especially when there are kids involved."

"I know and admire that trait in you." He smiled, savoring the fiercely protective glance she directed toward her giggling children and suddenly wishing she was the mother of the child he didn't know, the one he'd abandoned.

With a mother like Sophie his child would be deeply loved because that's what Sophie did. Of course, if she was his child's mother, Tanner was pretty sure she wouldn't allow him within fifty feet of their child. Sophie would be as protective as a mother bear of her cub.

"I suppose the responsible thing to do would be to investigate, make sure mom and child aren't starving in some hole, or living on the streets," she finally agreed, brown eyes dark and brooding.

He nodded. "Agreed."

"Maybe the woman's married now, with a family. If the kid is fine, the least selfish thing this guy could do is to not disrupt their lives and get on with his own, preferably doing something that will make a difference in the world and maybe help make up for his past mistake."

Tanner gulped at the distaste lacing her voice. What would she say if she knew he was trying to do that by turning Burt's idea into reality? And yet, he didn't think this was only about Sophie's repugnance toward some nameless man who'd abandoned his child. Something in her tone said there was more to the antagonism behind her stiff words.

"You sound really angry toward my friend," he said in a quiet tone.

"If I do it's because I know what it's like to be on your own, the only one your kids can depend on," she said, still bristling. "Can you imagine what it feels like to know you haven't got a cent and no way to make one but know that in half an hour your child will be hungry and you have no way to feed him?" Her face tightened. Her voice broke slightly and she paused to regroup. "That even if you can find something for that meal, there's tomorrow and tomorrow after that to worry about? I hope you never know that helpless feeling, Tanner." Her hands fisted.

"That's how Marty left you." In that moment he understood the scared lurch of her voice and the passion behind her words. Sophie was still afraid. "You were left alone with two kids to feed, clothe and house. That must have been terrifying."

"Yes." She bowed her head, as if ashamed to admit it.

"I'm so sorry," he said as he touched her shoulder. "I wish I'd been there to help you through that. But at least you could count on God."

"Could I?" She studied him for a moment before her gaze veered away to study something in the distance.

"Of course you could." He was suddenly uncertain, given the flash of anger through her dark eyes. "You're here. You made it. You and the kids."

"Thanks mostly to the food bank." She lifted her head. Defiance blazed from her face. "If it hadn't been for that, we'd have starved."

"And the church." He saw something blaze across her face. "Oh, Sophie," he groaned. "You did tell someone at church, didn't you?"

"Of course not." Sophie glared at him. "Do you think I wanted the congregation talking about us, choosing the silly, clueless mom and her kids as their newest charity case?"

"Sweet, sweet Sophie." Tanner brushed his fingertips against her cheek, touched by her independence but frustrated by her attitude. "Is that what *you* think when you take your trays of leftovers to folks who need them?"

She frowned. "How do you know about— Davy," she breathed in an exasperated tone.

"Would you think of Edna, whom you help, as stupid or silly because she's fallen on hard times?" he asked. "Is that why you're over at her house taking care of things while she's in the hospital?"

"Davy talks too much," she mumbled.

"Or do you help," he continued, ignoring her comment, "because you see someone who just needs a hand, which you're glad to offer because it makes you feel as if you matter, as if someone needs *you*?"

"It's not the same." She winced at his bark of laughter. "Okay, it's quite a bit the same but back then I had to stand alone, to solve my own problems."

"Why? That's completely against the whole point of faith." Tanner frowned.

"Huh?" She stared at him as if he had two heads.

"By definition faith is trusting in something you can't explicitly prove. Or if you prefer a biblical definition, Hebrews eleven, verse one says 'faith is the assurance of things hoped for, the conviction of things not seen.'" He grinned at her, wishing he could hug her and watch those brown eyes lose their shadows. "In other words, believing God has it taken care of so you don't have to fuss about it."

"Tanner, that sounds good but practically it makes no sense." She glanced at her kids. "That's like saying I should let Davy and Beth climb this wall without any advice or protection because God will watch out for them."

"I'm not saying that. I'm saying the *worry* is

unnecessary." Tanner sought to explain himself. "Faith is saying 'I can't be here all the time for my kids but I've entrusted them to God and I trust Him to do His best for them when I can't.' It's leaving the results up to God."

"Is that what you do?" she asked, her forehead marred by a frown, her voice hesitant.

"Not all the time," he admitted shamefacedly. "Sometimes I try to work things around to ensure the result I want and then something I didn't foresee happens and I wish I'd left it up to God." He winced at her nod. "It's a journey, Sophie. I'm learning to walk by faith. I still make mistakes."

"I tried that," she admitted in a whisper-soft voice, her head bent. "After I got married, I promised God I'd do the best I could if He'd be with me." She lifted her head and looked directly at him, her brown eyes welling with tears. "He wasn't."

"Of course He was." Tanner's heart ached for the doubt that plagued her. "In Second Timothy it says, 'Even when we are too weak to have any faith left, he remains faithful to us and will help us.' That proves how much God loves us."

"But I never *feel* like He's near, Tanner." Sophie's big brown eyes shone with tears. "I always feel like I'm alone."

Her raw whisper got to him. With a groan for her pain, Tanner gave up restraining himself and pulled Sophie into his arms, stunned by how right it felt. "He's always right beside you, sweetheart. Always leading you, always guiding you."

"Even when He let Beth…be the way she is?" Sophie's hesitant whisper came as she lifted her head to search his gaze for reassurance.

The satin strands of her hair brushed against Tanner's cheek, carrying the faintest scent of lilac and bringing feelings of affection and comfort and belonging. Of Sophie.

"Honey, Beth is a living testament to faith. She's vulnerable and yet there's this trusting spirit inside her that allows her to trust God in a way that makes me envious." Tanner pressed his forefinger under Sophie's chin so she had to look at him. "God knew exactly what He was doing when he created Beth. She's His gift to us."

"That's what I think, too," Sophie murmured. "But sometimes—"

"Sometimes you let fear take over," he said softly, brushing a hand against her smooth cheek. "And that opens the door to doubt. That's when you have to cling hardest to your faith. God is here. He will do his best for us. Count on that, Sophie."

As her intense brown eyes locked with his, Tanner couldn't tamp down a rush of affection for this woman. She was so strong, forcing her way through her misgivings to be the mom her kids needed. What was this need inside him, to be here for her, to protect and support her—why did he feel compelled to protect Sophie Armstrong?

She was so beautiful, so utterly lovely inside and out. His arms tightened around her. He needed to get closer. He dipped his head—

"Are you going to kiss Mama?"

Pulling away from Sophie, Tanner called himself an idiot. Was he so desperate to be part of a family, to share his life and his work with someone who could understand and support him, that he would kiss Sophie in front of her kids?

*Yes!* his spirit groaned.

"I'm glad you finally left those rabbits to come over." Tanner dropped his hands to release Sophie and fought to control his voice. He winked at Beth. "You can tell me what you think of my climbing wall." That reminded Tanner that his goal was to fulfill Burt's dream by reaching kids—which superseded any personal wants.

Trouble was, the more Tanner worked with Sophie, the more his yearning grew to be part of a family, preferably a family with a mom like her! His skin reacted to her hand when it rested fleetingly against his arm with a burst of electricity.

"Thank you, Tanner," she murmured too quietly for the kids to hear. "I'll look up the verse tonight. Maybe some Bible study will help rebuild my faith in God."

Tanner was surprised by just how much he wanted that for Sophie. But caring meant he was getting too close to her. He had to stop trying to get his own desires. The thought made him grin.

Faith was sure easier to preach to Sophie than it was to live by.

## Chapter Seven

"I can't believe I let you talk me into this." Tanner's visible gulp as he surveyed the twenty-odd kids who were mounted up and impatiently waiting for their trail ride to begin made Sophie smile. "There are way more of them than I expected."

"They're just kids wanting to learn to ride," she encouraged. "You've done that before. And Moses will be there as well as two of your hired men." Sophie hid her smile at Davy's proud stance on his horse, confident of his skill when his classmates were not. "And Davy will help, too."

"Nice to hear you have faith in your son." Tanner studied her for several moments before lifting his reins. "Does your trust extend to me?"

Sophie wasn't going to answer that because she didn't have an answer. She was comfortable with leaving her kids in Tanner's care. She knew he'd protect and care for them. But trust him? That was asking a lot more than she could give.

She swerved her gaze away, stepped back and watched Tanner lead the way over the trail. Davy's school class followed in pairs, their teacher in the middle with Moses, and two of Wranglers' hands in the rear. It was the first large trail ride Tanner had attempted and he was doing it mostly because Davy's teacher, after noting a huge change in him, hoped Tanner could make her science project on animals come alive for the rest of her class.

*Please, please let everything go okay*, Sophie prayed. It was the first time in ages that she'd actually asked God for something. *Now have some faith*, she reminded herself. Faith. That was the hardest part.

"Why couldn't I go on the horses with Davy, Mama?" Beth's usually happy face drooped with disappointment.

"You can go another time, sweetie. This time is for Davy's class to have a riding lesson." She tried to soothe her daughter but Beth wasn't in a soothing mood.

"I wish I had school friends to ride horses with," her daughter muttered before turning toward the house.

"You don't like being homeschooled?" Sophie asked, surprised by Beth's discontent. She struggled to quell the rush of hurt she felt. She'd tried so hard…

"I love you, Mama." Beth hugged her tightly and pressed a kiss against her arm. "I like being with you, too. But I want lots of friends like Davy has."

"What about Bertie and Cora Lee?" Sophie sat down on Tanner's patio and patted the seat next to her for Beth to also sit, probing this uncertain territory with a worried heart.

"They're nice but I want more friends. Lots of them. And I want to sing in the kids' choir." Beth's lips pressed in a firm line that warned Sophie she wasn't about to be swayed.

"Still?" Sophie's heart sank a little at Beth's swift nod. Her daughter was so not musically gifted.

"I want to sing songs to God like that lady and her girl did on Sunday." Beth leaned her head against Sophie and sighed. "I know I don't sing very good, but I could learn, Mama. I could try really hard to learn."

"Oh, honey, I know you'd try." Sophie drew her sweet child into her arms and held her, trying to soothe what could not be soothed. Beth couldn't sing.

After a moment Beth drew away so she could look at Sophie, blue eyes sad. "Remember that book we read about the lonely puppy. I think I'm like him, Mama. I'm lonely."

The words cut a swath straight to Sophie's heart. She'd tried so hard to do everything right for this precious child, to protect her from the scathing hurt of other kids who didn't understand her disability. Instead she'd made Beth feel isolated.

"Do you mean you want to go back to school?" she asked in a careful voice as fear bubbled up inside. How could she protect…

"No." The answer burst out of Beth, accompanied by a swift shake of her head.

"But you just said— Why not?" Beth's sudden retreat puzzled her.

"I shouldn't have said anything." Her blond head drooped.

"Why not?" Something was going on.

"Davy said I'd hurt you if I asked." Beth's bottom lip quivered and a tear rolled down her cheek. "I did, didn't I? I don't ever want to hurt you. I love you, Mama." She wrapped her arms around Sophie's waist and squeezed.

"Well, I love you, too, sweetie. That won't ever change. But I want you to tell me why you don't want to go back to school." She saw several emotions vying for supremacy on Beth's expressive face. Finally her daughter spoke.

"I don't want to go 'cause I'm too dumb just like Bertie said." Beth hung her head.

"Honey!" Appalled, Sophie lifted her chin to peer into her eyes. "You are not dumb."

"Bertie said the other kids say that's why I can't go to school anymore. They said you have to teach me 'cause I'm too dumb to learn at school." Beth began to weep as if her heart was broken. "I don't want to be dumb. I want to go to school like Davy."

"Oh, Bethy, I don't think you're dumb." Sophie tamped down her anger at the slur, comforted her child and searched for a way to handle her daughter's unhappiness. "But actually I'm glad you told me because I've been thinking it's time for you to get back in the school. I homeschooled you because I didn't think you were happy at school. But you're older now and you need to be among your friends. I was just waiting for you to be ready."

"But I don't want you to be sad," Beth protested.

"Why would I be sad?" Sophie couldn't figure it out but she had a hunch Davy had something to do with this. Beth's next words rendered her speechless.

"Because if I go to school you'll be all alone with nobody. Davy said that I shouldn't say anything because when I'm at home you don't worry so much." Beth sniffed. "Davy and me don't like it when you worry, Mama."

So she was causing problems for both her kids. Sophie cringed inside. Davy must have guessed she hadn't removed Beth from school only because she was struggling but mostly because she'd heard the horrible taunts of other kids and wanted to save Beth from unhappiness.

"I can do it, Mama. I can learn at school." Beth's blue eyes implored her to understand while confirming Sophie's realization that her children understood far more than she'd given them credit for. "Anyway I don't care what other kids say about me."

"You don't?" she asked, stemming her tears.

"Nope. You love me and Davy loves me and God loves me." Her daughter's sweet smile lifted Sophie's hurting heart. "God will help me. That's what He does. He helps people who need him." Beth's trusting words added to the lump inside Sophie's stomach.

*A child shall lead them.*

"If we trust God to help us, He does, Mama. That's what Pastor Jeff said."

Each word was a prick against Sophie's heart. *Trust.* Beth trusted God but her mother couldn't? Humbled and ashamed, she realized that not only hadn't she trusted her sweet child, she hadn't trusted God to protect her daughter, either. She wasn't the example her daughter needed.

"I'm sorry I hurt you, Mama." Beth's hand touched her face, trying to soothe pain she hadn't caused.

"You didn't, darling. You make me very proud. I love you, Bethy." Sophie hugged her daughter tightly. "I'm sorry I didn't trust you," she whispered against Beth's flaxen head. "I'm so sorry."

And Beth, being Beth, immediately forgave her.

*This is what your refusal to trust brings*, a voice inside her head chided. *When are you going to trust God? He loves Beth even more than you do.*

"Mama?" Beth wiggled to get free. "When are Mr. Cowboy and Davy coming back?"

"Soon," Sophie said after checking her watch. "Want to help me get things ready?"

"Sure." Beth trailed beside her into the house. "Then we can talk more about me singing." She tilted her head to peer into Sophie's face, her concern visible. "Are you worrying, Mama?"

"No, sweetie," she said past the lump in her throat. "I just want you to be happy."

"I am." Beth did a pirouette, eyes shining with joy. "I'm always happy."

"I know." *Why aren't I?*

And then Tanner's image slid through her mind

and an effervescent giddiness began bubbling inside. He was such a great guy. Thinking about him made her happy. And it shouldn't.

As Sophie worked to assemble lunch, she had to remind herself that these soft feelings for Tanner had to be routed. He was committed, caring and determined to fulfill Burt's dream. That was great. But there could be nothing romantic between them.

*Because you won't trust him?* her brain demanded.

"I can't," she whispered. "I just can't take that risk again."

Trusting in others had ended badly before. No matter how much she admired Tanner Johns, Sophie could not get past those memories.

"It seems I keep repeating this, but thanks again for serving a great lunch, Sophie. Those pizza bun things were delicious." Tanner waved as the school bus filled with happy kids pulled out of the yard. "I think Davy's classmates had a good time *and* learned something."

"I'm sure they did." She edged away from him and entered the kitchen, distracted by the way her pulse leaped whenever he was near. "Davy said you made it very interesting. And of course he loved Moses's spiel. History seems to be growing on my son."

"What's wrong?" Tanner gripped her arm so she had to face him. "I know something happened because Beth kept peeking at you with a worried look. So tell me."

"It's nothing important. Just—I'm sending her back to school." There. She'd said it. And now she felt like a part of her lay exposed and raw. "I've done the best I could these past months. I think she's learned a lot. But it's time for her to return to school."

"And that bothers you." He poured himself a cup of coffee and sat down. "Why?"

Sophie glanced toward the patio to check Beth's location, not wanting her daughter to overhear her fears.

"She's gone with Moses to see a new calf." Tanner patted the chair next to him. "Talk, Mama."

"I think I messed up by taking her out of school," Sophie admitted after she'd sat down. She sipped her coffee thoughtfully.

"Why did you do that?" he asked.

"I overheard some kids teasing her one day when I picked her up."

"Beth was upset?" Tanner's lips tightened. She loved him for caring so much.

"That's the odd thing. As I think back on it now, I don't believe it bothered her unduly. But it sure got to me. I was furious. I wanted to protect her," she admitted sheepishly.

"You wanted to punish the nasty kids," Tanner corrected and chuckled when she glared at him. "I think that's a mother's instinct. There's nothing wrong with that."

"Yes, there is." It hurt to admit it. Sophie set down her cup, picked up one of the cookies she'd made earlier and nibbled on its corner. A moment later she put it down. "I thought I'd decided to homeschool Beth to protect her, but actually I did it to make me feel better."

"Huh?" Tanner poured himself another cup of coffee, topped up hers, then returned to his seat across from her. He chose another cookie as he waited for her to continue.

"You might not realize it but I'm a bit of a control freak, Tanner." She frowned when he choked on his coffee, then coughed to clear his throat.

"*You* might not realize it, Sophie, but that's a bit of an understatement." His teasing amusement stretched a grin across his face.

"Okay. Make fun of me." Her face burned with embarrassment. "But my decision to homeschool has hurt Beth. I feel better when she's with me, but she doesn't. She's lonely and she wants more friends. I cheated her of that because I was too afraid to let her handle the teasing, the snubs and whatever else those kids dished out."

"Sophie, you did your best for her." Tanner's

hand slid over hers, warm and comforting. "That's what a mom is supposed to do."

"A mother isn't supposed to make her kid afraid to say what she wants for fear she'll make me worry." She pulled her hand from his, hating the knowledge that she'd failed her children. First Davy and now Beth.

What kind of mother was she?

"What are you really worried about, Sophie?" Tanner's quiet question surprised her. "Let me guess. You're afraid something will happen and you won't be there to protect Beth."

"Yes." She lifted her chin. "She's an innocent, Tanner. I don't want her hurt. Or Davy."

"But they will be hurt, Sophie," he said quietly. "One way or another life hurts all of us. It's part of living." He leaned forward to stare earnestly into her eyes. "You can't protect them from everything, and even if you could it wouldn't be healthy. Beth and Davy have to learn to deal with life's problems on their own. That's how they grow."

"It's just so hard to stand back and let it happen when I could prevent it," she murmured.

"Has preventing it made Beth happy?" He smiled when she shook her head, then reached up to brush the hair from her cheek so he could stare into her eyes. "Beth isn't alone, you know."

She frowned at him, enjoying the touch of his fingertips against her skin. "Meaning?"

"Beth and Davy are God's children and He loves them far more than you ever could." Tanner's soft voice oozed faith. "Whenever your kids encounter a problem, God's right there beside them, helping them through."

"Why doesn't He stop it?" she demanded, edging away from his touch because that familiar yearning to lean on him had started up again. "Why must they go through it?"

"Sophie, think back on your life. Would you prefer to be alone, without Davy and Beth?"

"No." She glared at him. "Of course not. They are my everything."

"But having two kids is hard on you. You went through a lot of suffering because you had two kids to care for, right?" He waited for her nod. "So wouldn't it have been better to have avoided all that by simply not having them or giving them away for adoption?"

She stared at him, unable to believe he'd said that. Then the light dawned. "You're saying sometimes the pain is worth it."

"Yes. Davy is quickly reaching the stage where you soon won't be in control of who he meets or where he goes." His voice rebuked her in a tender tone. "Isn't it smarter to give him to God and trust He'll keep Davy safe instead of fighting to control everything yourself?"

"You're single, with no family—at least not that I know of. How do you know so much about kids and parenting, Tanner Johns?" Sophie suddenly saw the big cowboy in a fresh light. "I think you're one of those men who are born fathers."

She smiled at his surprised look, then rose to clean up the kitchen. Tanner simply sat there staring at her as if she'd told him his cattle were dinosaurs.

"No, that's not it," he said in a choked voice, breaking a long silence. "That's not it at all. I'd be a lousy dad. I'll go check on Beth." He left, striding across the yard as if chased by a bull.

Surprised by his rapid departure, Sophie studied his disappearing figure and realized how alone the cowboy was. Despite a full slate of staff and his friendly interaction with anyone who came to Wranglers, Tanner somehow remained aloof. Because it just happened that way, or was that his choice?

*Get your mind off Tanner, Sophie, and clean up this mess. You have that anniversary party to cater tonight, remember?*

But her brain wouldn't leave the subject alone. When Tanner later waved her and Beth off, Sophie's last view of him was a solitary figure standing tall and strong, but alone.

She wondered what it would be like to live on Wranglers Ranch.

*With Tanner?* an inner voice asked.

She refused to answer it.

"Sophie's supposed to arrive soon with food for that Big Brothers group the church is bringing," Tanner said the following Friday, striving to mask the anger he felt. "Keep her and the kids away from here, okay, Moses?"

"Her boy won't like it," Moses reminded. "He likes to walk Goliath around this way."

"Not today. Tell Davy we need him to accompany the group on their ride. I'll clear it with Sophie." Tanner pressed his lips together. "Whatever you do, don't let anyone near this mess."

"You know who you ticked off that would do this?" Moses asked, surveying the charred remains of the old log cabin he'd been restoring.

"No," Tanner muttered but in the back of his mind he saw the face of Tige, a former street gang leader who'd been an addict back when Tanner had lived on the streets. Was their meeting in the grocery store yesterday coincidental?

A prickly warning he hadn't felt in ten years feathered up his spine. Was this fire Tige's doing?

"Ask Lefty to use the loader to clean this up, will you? He can scrape it right down so it looks like we're clearing a spot."

"Sure. The police?" Moses's arch look said the question was perfunctory.

"They're certain it was arson but found no clues so they're not hopeful about finding the culprit. Can you ask the boys to keep it quiet that we had some vandalism last night? We don't want to alarm anyone."

He waited for Moses's nod before walking toward the house, but he couldn't silence his brain from repeating the question uppermost in his mind. *What did I do wrong, God? Don't You want me to go for Burt's dream?*

It wasn't that he didn't trust God anymore, but they'd come so close to losing everything. Wranglers Ranch land was tinder dry. If he hadn't happened to wake up around two and smell the smoke…

Tanner checked that the wood was stacked and ready on the patio, the only safe place to have a campfire after the ride. Then he made sure the tack the group would use was in perfect condition. As he did his mind replayed the previous day's events.

He'd never expected to see Tige again, let alone in a grocery store. Nothing much had changed. Lulu still hugged his side like a leech, eyes glazed, blond hair stringy and thinner than Tanner had ever seen her. She was using. Tige was, too, though he was better at hiding the effect of his last fix.

"How are you, buddy?" Tige had slapped him on the back. Years ago that slap would have felled Tanner but he'd toughened up a lot since he'd been that helpless kid living on the street under Tige's auspices. "You still a cowboy?" he'd said, studying the boots and hat Tanner wore. "Musta stayed with that guy who kept hounding you, huh?"

"Yeah." Tanner hadn't wanted to give too much away. "And you?" Two kids hung on the sidelines. "These your babies?" He'd been astonished to see them so grown.

"Yeah. Teenagers are pests." Lulu had brusquely brushed off the two teens' request for money for a soda and Tige's language to them was no less rough. The boys had cowered away with shamed faces and scared looks.

Tanner's heart went out to them. How well he remembered feeling shrunken, worthless and afraid when he was with Tige.

"Good-looking boys," Tanner said with a smile in their direction.

"Think they'd make good cowboys, like you?" Tige's smile held no warmth.

"Maybe." The ice cream in Tanner's hands dripped with condensation. He held up the container to show them. "This is melting. I've got to go. Good seeing you."

"Yeah. Likewise. Hey, maybe we can get together, reminisce about old times, huh?" Tige's cagey smile had bothered Tanner but he'd pretended to be enthusiastic.

"Sure. Where you at now?" he asked.

"Oh, here and there. No fixed address, you know." Tige's face turned cunning. "You?"

Since Tanner couldn't lie he gave the best answer he could. "Same place."

"Still with Amy?" Tige's sly tone said he knew the truth.

"I haven't seen her since the day I left," Tanner said, keeping his face impassive. He held up the ice cream. "I'm getting soaked. See you around."

"Say, Tanner." Tige's fingers on his arm were not gentle. "Can you lend me a couple of bucks?" His eager look bounced from Lulu to the kids and back. "My check got held up."

"I haven't got much but I'll give you what I can." Tanner had been glad he'd left his wallet in his truck. "Let's see," he said, pulling his money from his pocket. "I've got maybe a hundred and twenty five after I pay for the ice cream. Will that—"

"You can have your ice cream another time, okay?" Tige had snatched all the money. "Thanks, buddy. Good seeing you." Clutching his cash,

Tige had hurried away with Lulu in tow. The boys looked uncertain as to whether or not they should follow until their mother bellowed. They gave Tanner a look that begged for help.

So he'd done something he probably shouldn't have.

"If you two ever need a break, come see me at Wranglers Ranch," he'd said in a very quiet voice, too quiet for their parents to hear.

Now, a day later, this fire told Tanner he should have kept his mouth shut. He felt certain Tige had something to do with it because he'd tried to interfere in Tige's business by talking to his kids. If his old street mate visited again it would be because he'd figured out that Tanner owned Wranglers. When that happened Tige wouldn't be satisfied with a measly hundred bucks.

Worried about visitors, but especially worried that Sophie and her kids could be in danger, Tanner had told the police investigators about his past association with Tige. They'd brushed off his concerns. They knew Tige, insisted he wasn't into arson. He was into drugs, lots and lots of drugs that hurt innocent kids and dragged them down to a life of misery. But arson? They'd shaken their heads.

"Tanner?" Sophie's voice drew him out of his reverie and back to the present. "Are you okay?" she asked, staring at his bunched forearms.

"Yeah. Sure." He forced his muscles to relax and smiled. "Can't a guy daydream?"

"Looked more like a nightmare from your scowl," she said with a frown. "What was your daydream about?"

"My birthday's tomorrow," he said, blurting out the first thing he could think of to evade that curious brown gaze. "March first."

"Really?" Sophie stared at him for several minutes as if she had trouble believing him. "You looked upset."

"You'd be upset, too, if you had only three more years in your twenties. I'm getting old." She didn't look convinced by his joking so Tanner didn't push it. He just wanted the conversation off himself. "Everything okay for the ride?"

"Sure. Except I didn't see any ice cream in your freezer." She kept looking at him as if she knew he was hiding something. "I thought you said you were going to buy a gallon yesterday."

"I forgot. I can go get it now," he said, eager to escape her too-knowing gaze. "What flavor do you need?"

"No, don't make a special trip." She grinned. "Actually I don't *need* it. I made different desserts than I'd planned, chocolate ones. We'll be fine without ice cream." She paused, then asked quietly, "Tanner, what's wrong?"

Thankfully he heard the chug of the church bus just then.

"There are our guests," he said, forcing enthusiasm into his voice. "Let's go greet them. Where are Beth and Davy?"

"Talking to Moses." Sophie eyed him uncertainly but offered no objection when he threaded his fingers with hers and led her toward the group.

Tanner liked the feel of Sophie's hand in his. At least she trusted him that much. For now—until she learned that associating with him might be a problem. That thought made him release her hand. He couldn't endanger sweet Sophie or her kids. Maybe it was time to think about hiring some kind of security to prevent another issue like last night's fire.

*Help me protect her and her children*, he prayed silently as the group assembled with their horses. *Please, God, don't let anything happen to Sophie.* His heart hurt at the thought.

When had Sophie begun to matter so much?

## Chapter Eight

"I can't believe you wrangled a birthday party at Wranglers Ranch without me guessing." Tanner's delight at church folks gathered on his patio warmed Sophie's heart. He thanked them, then asked her, "How did you manage this?"

"I had a little help while you were goofing off up in the hills today." She smiled at her ranch hand accomplices who led the guests to the pizza buffet line. "I hope I didn't miss inviting anyone who is important to you."

"Cowboys do not goof off," he said sternly, then smiled. "And everyone who's important to me is already here."

Tanner's soft, reflective voice and the way he looked at her made Sophie's stomach lurch and her heart race. Apparently only just realizing what he'd admitted, Tanner gulped, his Adam's apple bobbing as he did.

"I mean, it's very kind of you. Thank you, Sophie. I've never had anyone throw me a birthday party before."

Those words squeezed her motherly heart so hard her arms ached to comfort him. What kind of a life had young Tanner led not to have had even one birthday party?

"But Burt…?" she murmured, then dropped it when he shook his head.

"He'd take me out for supper and give me a gift." He grinned. "But I doubt Burt would have known how to throw a party. Guess that's why I never had one before."

"Then you must enjoy this one," she said firmly. But instead of dissipating, the crackling awareness she always felt around him thickened. Desperate to break it before she said something she shouldn't, Sophie resorted to teasing. "By next year you might be too old to enjoy another."

"And here I thought you were so nice." He shook his head sadly, gave a mock sigh, then headed off to get his own pizza.

"When can we give Tanner his gift, Mom?" Davy asked, Beth by his side.

"After we have cake," she promised, smiling at Davy's excited face.

What a change the big cowboy had made in her son's life. So much so that Davy had insisted on using most of the small salary Tanner now paid him for helping at Wranglers. Amazing to think that the money Davy hoarded to buy a skateboard had been willingly depleted to purchase a special pocketknife for the cowboy. Her son was at last learning about giving and caring, and Tanner was the reason. How could Sophie ever repay him?

But not just for Davy. When Beth had confided her desperate yearning to sing in the kids' church choir to Tanner, he'd taken that as his mission. Amazingly he'd found a voice coach with a reputation for successful work with Down syndrome children. Though now retired, Mrs. Baggle agreed to meet Beth. The two had immediately bonded. Mrs. Baggle insisted she would teach Beth for no fee. Sophie refused until the teacher finally admitted she'd always wanted to host an Easter Sunday brunch for her elderly quilting friends. Sophie insisted on catering it as payment.

Mrs. Baggle understood Beth's vocal issues but Sophie doubted Tanner knew how difficult singing was for those with Down syndrome or that the genetic disorder made the voice lower, which required more energy and training to produce sound. Years ago the doctors had told Sophie that Beth might never sing on key at all, and she'd feared Tanner would get Beth's hopes up for something that was impossible. She hadn't trusted him, certainly hadn't believed he'd find someone who not only taught her daughter to sing on key but encouraged Beth by making her feel her singing goals were reachable.

The voice lessons and a return to school had revitalized Beth. Sophie had never seen either of her children so happy.

Thanks to Tanner. And God answering her prayers.

If only she could finally learn to let go of the controls and trust Him.

"Scrumptious pizza. Thank you," Tanner said. Sophie had been so deep in thought she hadn't noticed he'd returned to sit beside her or that he'd finished eating. "I guess I'd better make a little thank-you speech—" His jaw dropped and his eyes opened wide. "You didn't," he whispered.

"Oh yes I did." Sophie laughed at his surprise as Moses carried the three-layer chocolate cake toward him. Atop thick chocolate icing sparklers glittered and twenty-six candles fluttered in the soft breeze.

Beth immediately led the group in a rousing, if off-key, rendition of the birthday song. Then Tanner's friends from church teased about his age and made a big fuss about his inability to blow out all the candles.

"Does that mean you're an old bag of wind?" one of his usher buddies gibed.

"No, it means Tanner has a girlfriend," Beth explained in her most serious voice.

Suddenly Sophie felt the intense stares of everyone on her. Her cheeks burned at the knowing looks. Tongue-tied, she couldn't think what to say. Fortunately Pastor Jeff broke the embarrassing silence.

"Are you going to share that cake or hide it away like you did those pies?" he demanded with a wink at Sophie.

Laughter rippled across the patio. Monica and Tiffany brought plates and forks and a huge container of chocolate ice cream. At Tanner's urging they took over cutting the cake and added generous scoops of the frozen treat. Davy and Beth passed around the filled plates.

"Enough chocolate for you?" Sophie asked, tongue in cheek.

"Almost." He licked his lips then frowned. "You shouldn't have hired staff for this," Tanner scolded. "I'll pay Monica's and Tiffany's wages."

"You certainly will not." Indignant, she glared at him. "This party is the Armstrong family's gift to you. Are you rejecting it?"

"Nope." He blinked and shook his head as he licked a blob of ice cream that was tucked at the corner of his lips. "No way. Burt didn't raise a dummy. I am going to thank you for it." He grinned and cupped a hand against her thrust-out chin. "Thank you, Sophie."

And then Tanner kissed her.

That kiss was over and done before Sophie could react, but she was acutely aware that every eye in the place was on them. As if she needed that with every nerve in her body already tingling from Tanner's kiss. She wished she could melt into the patio stones, and yet she wanted to replay that fraction of a second over and over, even knowing that now gossip about a relationship between them would run rampant at church. They didn't know a relationship with Tanner was impossible.

*But you want a relationship. Don't you?*

"Stop scowling, Sophie," Tanner whispered in her ear. "They're focused on the cake, not you."

Which was such a lie, but she loved him for it.

Wait a minute—loved him? No! She didn't love Tanner. She didn't even trust him.

And yet—was there anyone she'd ever relied on more than Tanner Johns?

"Mama, our presents *now*?" Beth's whisper nudged Sophie out of the fog she'd fallen into. She must have nodded because a moment later her daughter plunked the gift she'd helped wrap this morning in front of Tanner. "This is from Mama," she said with a big grin. "You open it first."

He opened the card, laughed at the joke, then carefully unwrapped the gift. For several long moments he studied the coffeemaker as if he couldn't quite understand it. Then Tanner lifted his gaze to hers and said, "Thank you," in a polite voice.

Sophie just smiled.

"There's more. Open my gift now." Beth handed him a wildly decorated bag she'd made. When Tanner didn't take out the contents fast enough she helped him, setting the six boxes of coffee pods in a row on the table in front of him. "These are to use with Mama's gift. Now you won't ever have bad coffee anymore, Mr. Cowboy."

It seemed to Sophie that everyone but Tanner understood how fitting the gift was because the entire crowd applauded.

"Now we won't have to make excuses not to drink his coffee when we come to Wranglers," Pastor Jeff called out. "Tanner can actually serve real coffee."

Seeing Tanner's confusion, Sophie leaned close and explained how the machine worked. "It makes a perfect cup of coffee every time," she assured him.

"Like you make?" he said, his breath brushing against her cheek, enhancing the intimacy of the moment.

"Probably better than mine." Realizing they were again the focus of everyone's attention, Sophie stood, desperate to put some distance between them so she could corral her wayward senses. "Later I'll show you how to use it," she promised and began collecting plates.

"Thank you, Sophie." The sincerity in his voice and the glow in his green eyes made her heart skip. Surely he wasn't going to kiss her again? She cleared her throat, desperate to get away and clear her head.

"I made the coffee tonight, not Tanner," she announced as Monica and Tiffany waited by the coffee cart. "I guarantee it's safe to drink."

As the group hooted with laughter, Sophie shifted away from Tanner. Some approached him to present their gag gifts while others headed for the beverage cart. All in all, she was fairly pleased with the way the evening had gone. She was about to go into the house when she saw Beth and Davy talking to two teenage boys whom she'd never seen before. Concerned, she approached them and heard Davy ask, "You mean you want to talk to Tanner? He's the one who owns Wranglers Ranch."

When the boys nodded, Davy hurried toward his hero.

"I'm Sophie. And you are?" She waited until the pair had exchanged a glance.

"Rod" came from one, followed by "Trent" from the other boy.

"We're having a birthday party for Tanner tonight. Would you like some cake?" She saw the direction of their eager gazes and added, "Or pizza?" At their nods she led them to an empty spot and motioned for Monica to bring two drinks while she retrieved a pizza.

Apparently starved, the boys gulped down several slices of the pie before Tanner appeared. Sophie saw surprise on his face.

"Trent and Rod would like to speak to you." Something in Tanner's manner made Sophie believe he wanted a few minutes alone with the boys. "Come Beth, Davy. We'll get some cake and ice cream for the boys. And maybe another drink." She shepherded her kids away to give Tanner privacy.

"Do you think those are some of the street kids Tanner talks to?" Davy asked with a backward glance.

"What do you mean?" Surprised, Sophie listened as she cut two large wedges of the remaining cake and handed Beth and Davy each a glass of iced tea to carry.

"Tanner finds kids who don't have a home or food. Sometimes he takes them for a hamburger," Davy said knowledgeably.

A flutter of worry about the big generous cowboy grew to a ripple. Tucson was mostly a safe city but still—a shiver tiptoed up her spine. "Does Moses go with him?"

"I don't think so." Davy frowned. "He told me not to say anything."

"I'm sure Tanner won't mind me knowing." Sophie led the kids to the table where the cowboy was holding an animated discussion with the boys, who vehemently shook their heads at whatever he was saying. Silence fell while she served the cake and drinks. "Eat up. If you want more, we have lots." Then with a smile at Tanner she gave her children jobs to help with the cleanup.

"Mama, are those boys friends of Mr. Cowboy?" Beth's face scrunched up in a frown.

"Why do you ask, honey?" Sophie paused to study her daughter.

"'Cause he's giving them money."

Sophie turned in time to see Tanner slip a bill into the palm of the oldest boy. Since Tanner didn't look upset or angry, she turned back to her work.

"They're leaving now. Mr. Cowboy is watching them. He looks sad." Beth dropped the paper she'd collected into the trash. "I'm going to give him a hug."

Sophie put her hand on Beth's shoulder. "Wait a minute, okay, sweetie? Give Tanner some time to himself."

"Can I pray for him?" her daughter asked, blue eyes glowing huge in her round face. "He's my friend. We pray for our friends, don't we, Mama?"

"That's a great idea," Sophie approved.

"'Kay." Beth sat down on a bench, bowed her head and began silently praying.

From the corner of her eye Sophie saw Tanner motion to Lefty and give him directions. The man hurried away and a moment later one of the ranch's four-wheel-drive vehicles left a cloud of dust as it took off down the driveway. Tanner turned and caught Sophie staring. He walked toward her.

Not wanting to intrude, she merely asked, "Everything okay?"

"They're two street kids whose parents are, I believe, abusing them. I met them in a store the other day when I saw an old—acquaintance." There was a pause before he said the word, as if he'd deliberately avoided saying "friend." "I told them to come here if they needed anything. They said they hadn't eaten today. Thanks for feeding them."

Sophie shrugged. "No biggie, as Davy would say. Feeding a kid is easy to do, not like trying to reach their souls, as you do on your street visits." She said it nonchalantly.

Tanner jerked as if she'd struck him. "How do you know—" Then he shook his head. "Davy."

"No secrets with kids around." Sophie sensed his reticence. "You don't have to tell me anything." She knew it was the right thing to say when he remained silent for a moment.

"I knew their father back in the days when I lived on the streets." He glanced around. "I need to mingle right now. But can I tell you about it when everyone's gone? You don't have to hurry home tonight, do you, Sophie?"

"It's Friday. No school and I don't have anything scheduled for tomorrow so I guess we could stay for a while," she agreed. "Go enjoy your party, Tanner."

"I am," he said, his eyes dancing. "Some parts more than others." His gaze rested on her lips.

"I need to check on Monica and Tiffany." Sophie said it quickly, feeling as if her face was on fire. "Excuse me." She hurried away, knowing he was watching her with that cute lopsided grin of his.

At the doorway she gave in to the urge to turn back and check. Sure enough, Tanner stood in place, watching her with those intense green eyes. But he wasn't smiling. He looked as if he were struggling with a decision. Then Beth tugged on his pant leg and he smiled at her.

Something was definitely bothering Tanner, and Sophie could hardly wait to learn what was going on.


"I dropped them off on Fourth Street, boss. That was as far as they'd let me take them."

"Thanks, Lefty, I appreciate it." Tanner watched

his foreman leave the patio while his mind swirled with questions about Tige.

He put away the questions to entertain his guests, but when they'd all left and he was finally alone, he sat down on a bench to think about Trent and Rod. Had Tige sent his kids with that story? Tanner didn't think so but—

"Davy and Beth fell asleep." Sophie's glance around the empty patio told him she was waiting for that talk he'd promised. He didn't want to tell her anything about his ugly past, but his conscience demanded Sophie know the risk her kids might be taking if things escalated with Tige.

*Are you going to tell her everything about your past? Including the child you abandoned? Because if you don't, you know that someday Tige will.*

He ignored the voice in his head.

"Let's sit down."

"Okay." Sophie shivered slightly, prompting his realization that the night air had cooled.

Tanner added a couple of logs to the fire still burning in the fire pit to ensure she'd be warm enough. "First of all, thank you for making this birthday so special. I appreciate all the trouble you and the kids went to."

"It was our pleasure." Sophie sat with her beautiful face lit by the dancing flames.

"About those boys. Trent and Rod are the sons

of a man I knew as Tige from my days of living on the streets." Tanner wanted to hurry through the past and avoid long-buried thoughts that still brought pain. "I happened to meet Tige the other day when I went to the grocery store."

"Happened to meet?" Her brown eyes narrowed. "That's odd, isn't it?"

"Yeah." He grimaced. "I don't believe in coincidences, either. Maybe word is getting out about Wranglers and he recognized my name. I don't know." He kept going, anxious to get it said. "He's not a nice man, Sophie. Neither is his wife, Lulu. For as long as I've known Tige he's been into drugs, selling and using, friendly when he's high, mean and nasty when he's not. Anyway in the store that day I noticed his kids seemed ill at ease and I felt sorry for them. I told them to look me up if they ever needed anything. I guess that's why they showed up today."

"Because they were hungry." Sophie sat silently watching him, her face impassive. Finally, her voice very soft, she asked, "Why are you telling me this, Tanner?"

"That day I met him—Tige hit me up for some money." He exhaled, hoping, praying she wouldn't grab her kids and run when he explained. "The morning after I saw him I found a fire blazing in one of the old buildings Moses has been restoring. Understand that there was no electricity, nothing in there that could have caused a fire. Yet it burned hot and fast." He could see she didn't understand his inference. "The police insist it is arson but they found no clues as to who lit it."

"You think Tige did it." Awareness dawned, then she frowned. "But why?"

"As a kind of message that he's watching me. At least that's how Tige used to operate." Tanner couldn't shake the black mantle of dread. "He used to pass out what he called 'warnings,' maybe a beating, maybe something else equally nasty, to let you know that he was always watching."

"And if you didn't do what he wanted?" Sophie whispered, her pupils wide.

"His usual modus operandi was violence to make sure you did." Now came the hard part. "His sons are scared." He condensed what the boys had told him. "Apparently Tige and Lulu got high after I saw them. Those boys hadn't eaten for ages. They know they'll get in trouble if Tige finds out they came here, but they had nowhere else to go."

Tanner noticed Sophie didn't ask him about Children's Services or any other agency. Was that because she trusted him to do the right thing? But Sophie didn't trust.

"So now you're worried about us," she guessed. He nodded, sobered by concern. "What will Tige do if he finds out you interfered with his kids?"

"Tige only goes after someone if there's a profit for him." Tanner saw her absorb that. Her eyes expanded in understanding.

"You mean—he'll ask you for money when he learns you own the ranch?"

"Yes." Tanner exhaled. He hated saying this, hated distancing himself from this woman he admired. But the thought of Sophie, Davy or Beth being hurt because of him was intolerable. "I don't know if you and the kids should come to Wranglers anymore."

"We have to!" She stared at him. "Unless you have someone else in mind to cater the camp next week? And the Easter morning sunrise ride?"

"No, but—"

"It's my job, Tanner, and I don't quit on a job. Ever." She leaned forward, covered his hand with hers and squeezed. "Isn't the whole purpose of Wranglers Ranch to minister to needy kids?"

"Yes." Fear churned in his gut, eating away his resolve. He had to protect her. "But what if—"

"You're always after me for not trusting." Sophie's beautiful smile curved her lips. "This time it's you who isn't trusting, Tanner. Think about those two boys. They know Tucson's streets because they grew up on them, right?"

Tanner nodded though he didn't get where she was headed.

"You're trying to help street kids. Maybe this

is God's way of easing your foot in the door for this ministry." Sophie tilted her head to one side, thinking it through as she spoke. "Maybe Trent and Rod are the first steps in your outreach program for Tucson's street kids. Possible?"

What a woman! Not only did she chide him for his doubts, she saw past the immediate problems to the possibilities. How could he keep away from her? He couldn't.

Tanner leaned forward and brought his lips to hers. The kiss began lightly but quickly took on its own life, rapidly escalating into something more meaningful as Sophie wrapped her arms around his neck and tilted toward him. She kissed him back in a way that made Tanner certain she must have some kind of fond feeling for him.

A burst of yearning flared inside him. This woman felt so precious in his arms, like a wonderful gift he could never deserve. Tanner wished for more than a simple kiss but he didn't want to ruin the friendship she'd trusted him with. He was not going to repay this giving, caring woman by deepening the embrace, by asking for more than she could give. Sophie didn't want a personal relationship. She'd told him that. He'd respect her wishes no matter how much he hated letting her go. Besides, he didn't deserve Sophie.

Carefully Tanner eased away from her.

"What was that for?" Sophie whispered. She looked as shaken as he felt.

"Just—because." He pushed her soft brown hair off her face. "Because you're an amazing woman with amazing vision and amazing talents."

"Tanner, I cook. Hardly amazing," she scoffed.

"You don't just cook, Sophie. When you offer food, you meet a need by seeing into a person, past the barriers they put up to the hurting place inside them that aches to have someone care." He was saying too much and he knew it, but Tanner couldn't stop. "You can't pretend that you don't go over each menu for Wranglers very carefully, making sure it fits the ranch and whatever occasion you're serving. That detail and caring is evident in everything you do, from loving Davy and Beth to maintaining a house you don't own."

Afraid he'd said too much and given away how deeply he admired her, Tanner clamped his lips together and visually dared her to deny it.

"Thank you." To his surprise Sophie's eyes welled with tears. She squeezed his hand before letting go. "Thank you for saying that."

"It's the truth. You're a very special lady, Sophie Armstrong." Her gaze met his and somehow got tangled. For a brief moment, a yawning space in time, Tanner felt like he could see into the heart of the woman behind that brown-eyed gaze, who took on the world without complaint.

Then her lids dropped and hid her thoughts.

"I wish you'd tell me more about your past, Tanner." Her eyes narrowed and her voice dropped to a wistful tone. "If I knew more about your time on the street, maybe I could better understand why you're so worried about this Tige and what he might do."

"I don't like to remember that time." Tanner ripped his gaze from hers, afraid she'd see how much he feared her knowing the whole truth about his past. He blinked when her fingertips brushed his cheek.

"I'm sorry. I don't want to bring back any bad memories for you," Sophie whispered. "I just want to help you."

"You've already helped me a lot." He felt like a traitor. Was it lying if you kept a secret like his? *Yes!* his brain yelled. "One day I will tell you all about Tige and my past," he promised. *And then she'll walk away from you.*

"I'll hold you to that," Sophie promised, though questions remained in her dark eyes.

How Tanner wished he could be totally honest with her. But he kept hoping that with time she'd come to know him better, trust that he wasn't the total jerk his decision back then seemed to make him; that if Sophie knew who he was in his heart she'd be willing to forgive him his youthful mistake. Maybe.

"But what are you going to do now? Because I'm not about to walk away from my commitment to help you and Wranglers Ranch," Sophie said in a firm voice. "I believe that through you, Tanner, this place is going to reach a lot of kids. There's no way we can let one messed-up drug addict stop God's work."

*We.* Tanner smiled. He liked knowing Sophie was on his side. Liked it a lot. But Tige—what was he supposed to do about Tige? *Lord?*

"I will hire a security firm tomorrow." He frowned as he studied her. "But I'm not sure that's enough. I can't guarantee your kids' safety when they're here, Sophie."

To his astonishment she smiled.

"What's so funny?"

"Not too long ago, I'd have insisted I was perfectly capable of caring for my kids," she told him with a chuckle. "Or I'd have hightailed it out of here and shuttered them up at home regardless of how they protested."

"You're not going to do that?" He knew before he asked that she wasn't. "Why not?"

"A certain man recently rebuked me about my faith, or rather my lack of it." Sophie chuckled at his sheepish look. "I'm glad you did. Your words made me think about my claim to be a Christian.

I was really convicted when I read a verse in First John that says, 'If we are afraid, it is for fear of what He might do to us and shows that we are not fully convinced that He really loves us.' I've been living in fear, Tanner."

"And now you're not?" His brows drew together.

"Oh, I'm still afraid the sky will fall on me," Sophie joked, but the shadows in her brown eyes told him it was true. "I haven't gotten rid of that monkey on my back so easily. But lately I'm realizing how my lack of faith in God hurts me. And my kids. So I've been trying to work out my faith, or rather to let God work it out, by relinquishing my control."

"How's that going?" He didn't have to ask. Tanner could see by the look on beautiful Sophie's face that she would far rather cling to the reins of running her own life. His heart empathized at the difficult lesson of true faith in God that she was learning.

"It's not easy," she said in a low voice.

"Not supposed to be, honey. Trust is a process, one step at a time." He couldn't stop staring, appreciating the way she thrust out her chin, determined to trust no matter how much she hated it. "It gets easier, Sophie," he promised.

"I hope so." This time she didn't look away, didn't immediately end that sensitive current that zipped back and forth between them. Instead she studied him with an almost tender scrutiny. "Do you realize that you conducted your first real out-reach tonight, Tanner? And you didn't even have to leave the ranch."

He blinked, stunned to realize that it was true. He'd invited Tige's kids to come without even thinking. Tonight he'd talked to them as a friend, not as the preacher he'd figured he was supposed to be. "It seemed to come naturally," he muttered, awed by the insight.

"That seems like the best way." Sophie grinned at him. "Congratulations."

"Thanks." He savored the moment, delighted to have her there to share it. But the reality of the situation returned like a wet blanket. "But what about Tige?"

"What about him?" Sophie straightened her shoulders and met his look with a stern one of her own. "He's nothing to me. We've never met. Why should he care about me or my family?"

"I don't know." Troubled, Tanner frowned. "Tige was never exactly rational…"

"Listen." Sophie wrapped her fingers around his arm and squeezed, catching and holding his attention. "In learning to trust I've begun to understand that I have to live in the now or I'll drive myself crazy with what-ifs. Let's just keep working toward Burt's goal and trust God to work things out. Let's 'fan into flame the gift that is within you.'"

"I still don't know what that is," he complained.

"You'll figure it out." She smiled a Mona Lisa smile. "I think I have."

"Oh." He hoped she'd tell him what his gift was but she remained silent, though her eyes glowed with some inner secret. "Thank you, Sophie," he murmured, returning the pressure of her fingers against his.

"For what?" She tilted her head to one side.

"Everything. The party. Making every guest feel welcome. Making me feel special. For helping me make Burt's dream come true. For being you." Without even thinking he leaned forward and kissed her again. It felt so right to have Sophie here at the ranch, by his side, being his partner.

*She wouldn't be here if she knew why you're so afraid of Tige, especially of what he could tell her. Sophie wouldn't stay if she knew you walked away from your child and never looked back.*

Brought back to reality by that warning voice, Tanner helped Sophie pack up the kids while resolve filled his head. Along with hiring security for the ranch he would hire a private detective to find his child. Wranglers Ranch and the message of God's love was too important to be sidetracked by a man from his past. If he told her, Tanner was certain Sophie would agree.

The voice in his head laughed at him for believing Sophie would ever condone his past actions. If she knew what he'd done, she'd probably hate Tanner for abandoning his child.

*Please don't let Sophie hate me.*

# Chapter Nine

"I don't like the look on your face." Sophie tamped down the frisson of excitement that always fluttered across her skin whenever she was near Tanner. "Can you fix my oven or not?"

"Probably not," he muttered in disgust as he squeezed out from behind the appliance. "We'll find out when you turn on the breaker."

She did that, then returned to find him scowling. "Nothing?"

"Dead as a doornail. Sophie, the thing is older than time. You need a new one. Can't the person you rent from see that?" Obviously frustrated, Tanner gathered up his tools. "Why didn't you use the stove at the ranch?"

"I did use it for your Easter sunrise ride this morning," Sophie reminded him, wondering why she couldn't rid herself of this feeling that Tanner wasn't telling her something about his past.

She'd felt it again earlier when she'd asked him if he'd heard from Tige and he'd brushed her off.

"You used our kitchen to great success." Tanner patted his stomach, smile back in place. "Your cooking was so delicious that I've decided we'll have a sunrise service at Wranglers every Easter." He frowned. "So why didn't you take these cinnamon rolls there?"

"Because they were still rising while I was at Wranglers. Besides, Mrs. Baggle's place is only a few blocks away from here. It seemed silly to haul everything out to Wranglers and then back to my place. Also, how was I to know this thing would cease working today?" She glared at the old stove. "I don't have time to take the rolls to the ranch now. Mrs. Baggle's Easter brunch is going to be ruined and that's all she asked in return for teaching Beth."

"Mom, Mrs. Parker's home." Davy burst through the door, basketball clutched under one arm. "She's got a walker."

"A man is trying to help her up the stairs," Beth added.

"Edna." Sophie grinned and exhaled her relief. "Of course. Thank You, Lord." She closed her eyes, whispered a prayer of thanks and picked up the phone. After speaking to her elderly neighbor for a few minutes she wished her a happy Easter, then hung up. "Tanner, will you help me carry these pans next door?"

"Uh, yeah. Sure." His confused look made her giggle. But the cowboy's face rapidly cleared as he followed her across the backyard to her neighbor's house. "You're going to use her oven," he deduced.

"Yes, I am. Edna's homecoming is an answer to prayer." Sophie was surprised by how frequently it seemed God had answered her prayers lately. This Easter held more promise than she'd ever experienced. Was that because she'd been spending more time studying her Bible? Or because of Tanner?

Though Edna had just been released from full-time care and was still slightly pale, she seemed very mobile and utterly delighted to see them. Actually she seemed most excited to meet Tanner and clung to the cowboy's hand as she introduced her son, Ronald.

"He's a good son but he's like his father. Not handy at all," she complained. "I need a ramp to get in the door and Ronald doesn't know how to make one. Do you?"

"Uh, sure." Tanner handed the pan of rolls to Sophie and left to fetch his tools, Ronald following.

"Wow! Your Tanner's a hunk," Edna squealed when the door creaked closed behind them. "And so big and strong. It's good to have a man around, isn't it, dear? Didn't I tell you that?"

"Tanner's a good friend. I've been doing a lot of catering at his ranch," Sophie explained, embarrassed by her neighbor's garrulous appreciation of the cowboy. She hugged Edna. "You look good, Edna."

"I feel very well. It got much easier once I put my heart into doing the exercises. I was stubborn about obeying the physiotherapist." She twittered with laughter, then urged Davy and Beth to take a treat from the jar that seemed never to empty. "My, how you children have grown. Now, tell me about your mother's boyfriend."

"Boyfriend?" Davy frowned at Beth, then at Sophie.

"Tanner's not—" But she was drowned out by Beth, who was eager to share all she knew about the man who now seemed a permanent part of their lives.

But Tanner wasn't part of their lives. And Sophie couldn't let herself forget that, no matter how much she wished for more than friendship. She'd barely begun to trust God. Trusting a man was far more difficult, even if he was a man for whom she had increasingly strong feelings.

She'd tell Edna that later. For now she dashed between her neighbor's kitchen and her own, checking the food she'd prepared and sharing a smile with Tanner as he hammered and sawed under Ronald's gaze to form the ramp that would assist Edna.

Affection bubbled up inside Sophie. How many men would spend their Easter Sundays building a ramp for an old woman they didn't even know? Edna was right. Tanner *was* a hunk. And he was handy as well as very good-looking. He was also a good kisser.

She told herself to stop hoping that would happen again.

"It's time for me to deliver this food," she announced when the rolls were golden brown and oozing with sticky glaze.

"Leave the kids here with me," Tanner said. "They can help finish the ramp while you make your delivery." When she didn't answer he frowned. "Okay, Sophie?"

"Yes," she murmured, touched by his generosity. What would she do without Tanner's unstinting help?

It didn't take long to reach Mrs. Baggle's. There were eight older women waiting and they twittered and giggled like young girls as Sophie set out the brunch she'd prepared.

"Scalloped potatoes," Mrs. Baggle breathed. "I haven't had those for years. And baked ham with cherry glaze. How wonderful."

"I hope you enjoy everything," Sophie said as

she arranged napkins. She set a covered square container in the fridge. "The dessert crepes are in here, ready whenever you are, Mrs. Baggle." She had to smile at the other women's eager expressions. "Now, shall I make tea?"

"Oh, no, dear. We'll do that after we've eaten. Will you join us?" Mrs. Baggle nodded when Sophie declined the offer. "Of course you want to spend your Easter with Beth and Davy. And your nice boyfriend. Go now, dear. You can pick up your containers tomorrow."

"Thank you. Happy Easter," Sophie called as she walked out the door, neglecting to correct Mrs. Baggle about Tanner. After all, he *was* nice.

The ladies' cheerful "Happy Easter to you, dear" made her smile.

For the first time in a long time, it truly *was* a *happy* Easter. Thanks in large part to Tanner.

*I need to think of some way to thank him*, she mused on the drive home. But how? Tanner was rich. He sure didn't need anything she could buy.

Sophie was surprised to find the big cowboy sitting on her front step with her children when she pulled up in front of her house. The kids jumped up and hurried toward her.

"Tanner says we're going to the zoo," Davy said, obviously excited.

"Are we?" Her heart skipped a couple of beats when Tanner winked at her.

"We are," he affirmed. "We're just waiting for you to change out of your work clothes."

"Okay, then." She eased past him, trying to erase the memory of being in his arms by focusing instead on the joy of spending an afternoon of free time with him—which did nothing for her heart rate. "I'll pack a little lunch—" Tanner's hand on her arm stopped her short. His touch sent a zing of warmth through her body. She couldn't tear her gaze from his.

"No more cooking for you today, Sophie," he said firmly. "We'll grab something there."

"But—" She stopped when he shook his head.

"It's Easter, a time to celebrate the risen Lord. Let's enjoy the day He's made for us." It wasn't so much Tanner's words as the wistful expression she saw in his green eyes that ended her argument. She had no intention of refusing. In fact, she could hardly wait to get started.

Funny how she always thought of Tanner as a loner. Was that an aura left over from his former street persona? How she wished he'd open up to her about his past. What was so terrible that he had to hide it? Drugs? Theft?

"Sophie?" His hand on her arm drew her from her introspection.

"Sorry. I'll change and be right out." She moved away from his touch while noting how much she liked it. Too much. "Beth, do you want to change out of your Easter dress?"

"Why?" Beth looked shocked by the suggestion. "It's an Easter dress and this is Easter," she said logically.

"Indeed it is. And a most lovely dress it is, too. The zoo animals will love it." Tanner grinned at Sophie. "We're waiting on you."

They didn't wait long. Sophie took mere seconds to change into her favorite sundress, loosen her hair from the topknot she favored for work and spritz on a few drops of her favorite scent.

*For Tanner?*

She ignored that mocking voice in her head and joined the others, inwardly glowing at his approving smile. She accepted his helping hand into his truck and made sure her kids were belted in before fastening her own. On the drive to Reid Park Zoo, Davy and Beth chatted with Tanner about Pastor Jeff's short sermon that they heard this morning at Wranglers' sunrise service. As Sophie listened to Tanner's answers to their questions, she was struck by the solid faith of the cowboy's answers.

"See, the thing is, Davy, that we are the center of God's plan." Tanner caught her scrutiny and smiled at her before he continued. "He dreamed up the idea of us and made us His children, part of His family, just because He wants to love us."

"Even if we do bad things?" her son wondered.

"Even if," Tanner affirmed.

"But God doesn't like us to do bad things," Beth corrected in a grave tone.

"Nope. You're right." Stopped at a stop sign, Tanner reached behind Sophie and tugged Beth's ponytail with a smile. "He doesn't like that. But it doesn't stop Him from loving us. No matter what we do He loves us because we're His kids."

"Sometimes I don't feel like God hears me when I pray to Him." Sophie saw Davy shoot her a quick glance as if he wasn't sure he should have admitted that. If he only knew how often his mother felt the same!

"We all have times like that." Tanner's tone grew pensive.

"Even you?" Davy asked in an awed voice.

"Especially me," Tanner said. "That's when I remind myself that nothing can separate us from God's love. Nothing."

"Does it say that in the Bible?" Beth asked. Sophie hid her smile at her daughter's fastidious insistence on knowing biblical references.

"It does. I'll show you later," Tanner promised. "It says something else, too. It says in Deuteronomy that the Lord our God is faithful and will keep His agreement of love for a thousand lifetimes for people who love Him and obey His commands."

"A thousand lifetimes is a long time," Davy murmured thoughtfully.

"Our God makes big promises. And He keeps them," Tanner said.

The kids seemed satisfied with that answer and so was Sophie, though when she got the chance she was going to ask Tanner some questions about her own Bible study. His faith seemed so much more developed than hers.

Rubbing shoulders with Tanner, she wandered through the zoo beside him as the kids dashed ahead. Then they'd run back to be sure the adults hadn't missed anything. It was a warm afternoon filled with fun and relaxation, and Sophie savored the closeness she felt with Tanner.

"Time for lemonade?" At her nod he bought them each a glass of the chilly beverage and they sat at a picnic table to enjoy it. Davy and Beth kept running off only to return full of information about the next exhibit.

"They're having so much fun. Thank you for bringing us here," Sophie said when they were alone for a few minutes.

"They're good kids. I enjoy being with them." Tanner smiled at her. She would have liked to read his eyes but they were concealed behind his sunglasses. For once he'd left his Stetson in the truck. "I enjoy being with you, too," he added in a quieter voice.

"It's mutual," she said, struggling not to grin at him and reveal just how much she was enjoying this afternoon. "I don't think Burt could have picked anyone better than you to run Wranglers Ranch."

"That's debatable." He shrugged, then grinned. "But I'm awfully glad he entrusted me with his dream. It's a challenge that's truly worthwhile."

"I agree." Sophie inclined her head to study him. "I noticed someone carved his verse about you into a piece of beech wood and hung it in the barn."

"I did," he admitted sheepishly. "I don't want to forget the things he told me."

*"Fan into flame the gift that is within you,"* she quoted. "Do you know what that gift is yet?"

"Not a clue." His nose wrinkled. "I don't have any special gifts unless you count riding a horse. I can do that okay."

"A little better than okay, I'd say. Moses showed me all those rodeo trophies you won." Sophie liked the way he deflected compliments. In her opinion, Tanner Johns had a lot to be proud of and yet he didn't put on airs or try to impress. He just did what needed doing. "I think you have many gifts. But you don't think of them as gifts."

He leaned back with a frown. "Gifts like what?"

"The way you handle Tige's sons for one

thing." Sophie wasn't sure he wanted her to discuss that. After all, he'd spoken about his former friend only one time and that was to warn her. She'd offered him several opportunities since but he hadn't confided anything more, so his past remained a mystery to her.

Tige's two boys kept reappearing at the ranch. Tanner acted as if that was perfectly natural. He never questioned them about their parents, simply treated them as if they were visitors—the same as other kids who'd recently begun to drop by. He made sure the two boys were fed, taught them how to sit on a horse and answered any questions they had. And he always invited them to come back.

"Being with Rod and Trent doesn't take any gift." He shrugged it off. "They're just kids."

"Kids in a bad situation. Lots of people would try to get them away from their parents or convince them to run away," she began but Tanner was vehemently shaking his head.

"I would never do that without a very good reason," he said in a harsh voice. "Families are precious."

"See?" Sophie grinned and nudged him with her elbow while wondering why he was so adamant on the subject of families. Her questions about him grew. "That's what I'm talking about.

Everything you do is for the kids' sake. That's a gift."

Tanner made a rude noise.

"It's common sense. I'm a product of a foster home. Believe me I'm well aware that if Rod and Trent were put in foster care they could be better off. It could also be much worse."

"You've made sure they're okay with Tige and Lulu, haven't you?" she guessed and smiled when he shrugged.

"Judging parents isn't my mission. My mission is to help kids," he said, his voice unwavering. "That means gaining their trust and trusting them to know when to ask for help. And those two haven't. I think they're willing to come to Wranglers because I don't interfere."

"But it's not just those two. You have a gift with most kids, Davy included," she insisted. "I've seen the way you work with them after they fail at something they desperately want to do, like Davy trying to rope that calf the other day." She joined in his reminiscent chuckle, then sobered. "He was frustrated and ready to blow. You could have made fun of him or told him to practice. Instead you used that opportunity to teach him about patience. That's a gift."

Tanner let his sunglasses slide to the end of his nose so he could give her a rolling-eye look. "You're pushing the definition, Sophie."

"I don't think so. I think God is using you at Wranglers far beyond anything Burt could have imagined. God showed him those qualities in you—those gifts that you're fanning into flame." She stared into the distance thoughtfully. "I wish I had some kind of gift."

"You do!" Of course Tanner being Tanner, he raced to enumerate what he considered her gifts and compliment her. She cut him off.

"It's nice of you to say, but I don't have any real gifts," she murmured sadly. "I'm not the type of person God uses."

"Why do you think that, Sophie?" he asked quietly. "Why do you think God isn't using you?"

"Because I'm not fit. Because I can't quite trust Him." She hung her head, ashamed of the admission. "Not completely. I'm trying but—I'm just not there yet."

"Listen to me." He shoved his sunglasses to the top of his head, then took her hand in both of his. "Willingness to be used is what God looks for. Trust me, He is using you. And as He does you will learn to trust Him more and more. It's a process. Trust grows. The more we use it, the stronger it gets."

She stared at his hand holding hers and wondered for the hundredth time why Tanner Johns wasn't involved with someone. Were single women so foolish that they couldn't see beyond his humble cowboy demeanor and recognize his integrity and compassion?

*Maybe he's hiding something that you can't or won't see.*

Taken aback by that thought, Sophie immediately wondered if there was something about Tanner that when revealed would cost her. She liked, appreciated and respected him but…

Distrust moved in. Much as she hated breaking contact with him, she slid her hand from his while forcing a smile.

"Thank you for your encouragement." She watched her children dart from one animal enclosure to the next and admitted, "I know it's foolish but somehow depending on God seems like I'm abandoning my role as a mother. After all, I'm responsible for them. Leaving things up to Him seems like I'm letting go of the controls He's given me."

"You're not letting go, Sophie. You're being their mother in the best way you know how, by seeking His will," he said. "Then you act, trusting that He's directing you."

How did Tanner's explanations about God always make her feel better, as if she wasn't the failure at Christianity that she always felt?

"Recently I've been reading Isaiah. I've been struck by how much God yearned for His children to love Him." He shook his head as if he couldn't wrap his mind around why it should be so. "They were disobedient, they took other gods, they did exactly what God said not to and He had to discipline them. Yet there's such a longing in His words, begging them to restore their relationship with Him and to have their love again. Such love amazes me."

Sophie made a mental note to read Isaiah as Davy and Beth rushed back, finished their drinks and pleaded to move on.

As the afternoon waned, the children's restlessness gave way to quiet introspection as Tanner frequently commented about God's painstaking efforts to make His creation perfect. And always the big cowboy emphasized how much God loved His children. Tanner made God the father's love come alive.

Yet it wasn't so much Tanner's comments about family as the way he expressed them, combined with the lingering hugs he'd given Beth and Davy that bothered Sophie later that night when she sat alone in her living room.

She'd watched him as the kids raced away from him, into the house. She'd seen the loneliness wash over his face, felt his yearning to stay, to share her family.

Once more Sophie's questions about him ratcheted up. Why didn't he talk about his past? Surely he'd dated, fallen in love at least once?

Sophie's misgivings about Tanner came from concern that the rancher was hiding something she wouldn't like. She cared a lot about Tanner. But she couldn't get past the fear that trusting him would cost her dearly.

# Chapter Ten

Tanner sat on his patio in the May sunshine, nursing a fragrant cup of perfectly brewed coffee, utterly stunned by the contents of the manila envelope in front of him. As he read everything in his private detective's update, hope shriveled inside him. Now he could only stare at the small picture that had been clipped to the report, desperately struggling to formulate a prayer for direction, for something to end this despair clawing at him. Nothing came.

All he could think of was that his child was gone. He'd never know that person, never see his potential or hear *Hi, Daddy*. His insides squeezed tight with pain and loss.

*God?*

Tanner didn't know how much time passed before he jerked to awareness at the sound of a vehicle arriving. He rose, stuffed the papers into the envelope and stored it under a plant pot, tucking the picture into his back pocket. Something else to hide.

His heart lifted as he caught a glimpse of a familiar van. Sophie and the kids. But she was catering a Memorial Day dinner today. She wasn't supposed to be here.

Something must be wrong.

Surprised by how glad he was to see her again, though only last night he'd enjoyed a barbecue dinner at her house, Tanner suddenly realized that they now saw each other almost every day. Which was good and totally fine with him. It couldn't be too often for Tanner. Sophie and her kids felt like his family, the one he'd always wanted and now would never have. That secret was hardest of all to keep.

"Hey," he greeted, opening her door. She looked beautiful, as usual, though her lips were pursed in a thin line. "What's happening?"

"Not that stupid stove of mine." She frowned. "I hate to keep running to you—"

"Why?" he demanded, surprised by how much he disliked her saying that. He wanted her to need him. He'd have to think about that later. "Aren't we friends? Don't friends help each other?"

"Well, you certainly help me an awful lot." She sighed and slid out of the van.

*Oh, Sophie. If only you knew how much I love*

*helping you, being around you, touching you. Kissing you?* A kiss wasn't nearly enough to satisfy his longing to hold her.

"I'm not sure you get as much as you give," she said, her tone wistful.

"Do you hear me complaining?" Tanner asked.

"Not yet. Guess the treats I've been leaving in your fridge must be working." Sophie laughed when he licked his lips, then sobered. "May I please use your kitchen? Again?"

"Of course. Hi, guys." He grinned at Beth, high-fived Davy. "What needs carrying in?"

"I brought everything for the meal," she said, handing him a stack of bins. "I haven't got time to run back and forth. It's already eight and I have to serve at one thirty."

"Okay, you two, lead the way." He chuckled at Beth's delicate maneuvers with her bulging bag of salad fixings. Davy, on the other hand, wielded his two plastic tubs with such carefree abandon that Tanner caught his breath when they teetered dangerously, and held it until everything was safely stored on the kitchen countertop.

"This is going to be tight." A hint of panic laced Sophie's voice. She who never panicked. With practiced ease she slid a pan that held perfectly sliced roast beef into the oven, covered it and set the temperature to warm the meat.

"It's going to be as perfect as everything else

you make. And we're going to help you." He glanced at Davy and waited for his nod. Of course, Beth copied her brother. "What should we do first?"

"Can you peel potatoes?" she asked hesitantly, as if she thought he'd never used a knife on a tuber before.

Tanner gave her a look he meant to say, *You doubt my abilities*?

"Of course you can. You're Tanner Johns. You do everything well."

If she only knew. Tanner made no response except to return her smile.

"There's a bag in that yellow bin. Start peeling. Beth, you can whip the cream for my banana cream pie and Davy, you can chop carrots. Are you sure you don't mind?" she asked Tanner.

"I might have," he said, thinking of how desolate he'd felt only ten minutes ago and how her arrival had chased away his gloom. "But since I've just finished the most excellent cup of coffee from a wonderful machine someone gave me on my birthday, I'm in a very good mood."

He winked, relieved that for now the dark clouds had dissipated from his brain though he knew they'd return when Sophie and her family were gone and he was alone. Again.

Unable to constrain his need to touch her, he reached out to caress her cheek and whispered,

"Calm down, Sophie. We're going to help you make this meal amazing. Trust us."

Tanner didn't miss the way her forehead furrowed and her eyes narrowed at his choice of words. So she still found it hard to trust. Even him? Tanner was going to have to do something about that.

He'd thought about buying her a new stove. But then it occurred to him that Sophie would stop coming to Wranglers so often if she didn't need his kitchen. He wasn't about to end these sweet meetings. He enjoyed having her and the kids here too much.

"Make thinner peelings, please." Meeting his dour look, Sophie explained, "I know exactly how many potatoes I need. If you keep peeling half away I'll run out."

"Yes, ma'am." He saluted then returned to his work. But he couldn't stop watching as she moved around the kitchen, checking on Beth's progress, stirring the pie filling on the stove, encouraging Davy to keep going. "We have to do our best to help your mom make this a fantastic meal, kids."

"Why?" Davy frowned.

"Because this is a dinner for men and women who have worked to protect our country and keep it free," Tanner explained. "Some of them have even been injured, lost arms or legs or they have scars that will never get better."

"Why do they do it if they get hurt?" Beth turned off the mixer and waited for an answer while her mother checked the consistency of the cream.

"They do it so we can live here in peace. They do it so we don't have to fight people who don't like freedom." He watched them process that information.

"I don't know exactly what freedom means," Davy said with a frown. "You mean like we're not slaves or something?"

"Sort of. Freedom means we can live without someone trying to make us do things we don't want to do," he clarified.

"You mean like when Bertie wants me to kiss him and I don't want to?" Beth's question stopped Sophie in her tracks. She stared at her daughter in shock. Tanner chuckled at Mama Sophie's dismay. She frowned at him so he cleared his throat and continued.

"Yep, sweetheart, sorta like that." He couldn't look at Sophie or he'd start laughing again. "There are some people in the world who don't want us to be able to go to church, or live without someone telling us what to do. Some people want to take what other people have and keep it for themselves."

"Like Josh," Davy said, nodding.

"Who's Josh?" Sophie's voice squeaked. Tanner felt a rush of sympathy. She was probably hearing about these particular issues for the first time and beating herself up that she hadn't known earlier and protected them.

"A kid at school who takes other kids' lunch treats and eats them," Davy replied nonchalantly. "That's why I always ask for two snacks." He grinned at his mother, obviously delighted with his solution.

"Good thinking, buddy," Tanner encouraged because Sophie seemed speechless. "Anyway, veterans are men and women who work so other countries can't take what we have."

"Like our treats you mean?" Beth frowned in confusion.

Tanner had to laugh out loud at that.

"I'll explain later. Okay, honey?" Sophie pressed a kiss against her daughter's hair. "This whipped cream is perfect. Can you chop up some dill for the salad now?"

"Sure." Beth bent over the task cheerfully, her concentration on the herb.

"I think Tanner is trying to say that we can thank these men and women," Sophie corrected with a wink at him, "by giving them a nice meal."

Tanner felt the impact of that wink straight in his midsection. A second later he was swamped by a rush of guilt. She still thought the abandoning father he'd discussed with her was some unknown friend of his. He hadn't trusted her enough to tell her the truth.

Who was he to preach trust to anyone?

He worked steadily, doing whatever she asked while encouraging the kids in their jobs. Half an hour before the appointed time, Tanner sat in the driver's seat of the van with Sophie beside him.

"Are you sure this is the right way?" She checked a street sign, then her watch for the fifth time. "I'm going to be so late."

"No, you're not. There's the place over there. We came the back way. You need to trust me, Sophie," he teased, then inwardly grimaced. There was that word again.

"Yes, I do," she said. He couldn't move under her steady scrutiny. Finally she broke that stare. "Now if we can get it inside without spilling."

"Puhleeze, woman! Have some faith." Tanner shook his head in mock reproof. He climbed out of the van, took the heavy chafing dish with the beef from her hands and followed her inside the building. He made six more trips with the kids "helping."

In the kitchen, Sophie worked fast. Her two helpers had already arrived and had the beverages under control. Realizing he and the kids were now in her way, Tanner guided the children into the dining room where veterans were taking their places at the tables. He began taking orders for coffee, iced tea and water, including Davy and Beth as he chatted with each vet. Soon the two children were following Tanner's lead, ensuring each person had what he or she needed.

A minister Tanner didn't know said grace, then Sophie and her staff began serving. They worked quickly, Monica and Tiffany emptying the rolling cart as quickly as Sophie filled it. Tanner's admiration for her well-oiled operation grew as a murmur of approval flickered through the room, which now resonated with the delicious aroma of succulent roast beef. Someone invited him, Beth and Davy to sit at a table and moments later Sophie whisked full plates in front of them.

"Aren't you eating?" he asked, realizing a moment later that she wouldn't stop until her job was finished.

She moved through the room like the consummate hostess, refilling plates with a gentle brush to the shoulder, a soft, sweet smile and words he couldn't hear but knew would bring comfort. No one was left out of Sophie's generosity, he noticed, when men and women carried take-out containers. A man across the table said the meals would go to those veterans who couldn't participate in today's ceremony.

As quickly as a veteran's empty plate was removed by Tiffany, Monica replaced it with a towering slice of banana cream pie with whipped topping. Davy's eyes stretched wide when his mother set his pie in front of him though Beth only smiled and said, "Thank you, Mama," before she lifted her fork to sample hers.

When Sophie leaned over Tanner's shoulder, he couldn't help but inhale the fresh citrus scent of her hair as she handed him his pie. She turned her head to look at him and their gazes locked. Her lips were a hairbreadth from his. Tanner had to work hard not to lean slightly to the side and kiss her. As if she knew, she squeezed his shoulder and moved away quickly.

He ate his dessert in a trance, stunned by the depth of his yearning to be close to her, to be the one she turned to every day instead of only during emergencies. Sophie Armstrong was everything he'd ever imagined in a woman: warm, generous, kind, giving.

He was in love with her!

"You have the best ideas, Tanner." Sophie shifted a little on her comfy lawn chair under the shade of a mesquite tree and inhaled, letting go of the tension that had built up from the veterans' dinner and her stupid stove. "Thank you for helping me this morning and then inviting us to spend this afternoon at Wranglers."

"You're always invited to Wranglers Ranch, Sophie." The warm intimacy in his voice made her feel cherished. "You should take a break more often."

"What about you?" She shook her head. "I saw those three boys show up, heard them ask if they could ride your horses. You seemed to know them."

"Friends of Rod and Trent," he said in what Sophie considered a guarded tone.

"Oh." She pretended to study her pink toenails. "Have you heard any more from Tige?"

"No." He used Davy's squeal as he jumped in the creek to change the subject. "We've had another week of camp fill up. Two more and we'll have the summer filled."

"And you won't charge for any of them?" she asked curiously.

"No. Not unless we're asked to rent. Then I'll request a nominal fee." He smiled. "Don't worry, Sophie. Wranglers is well funded. Even if we weren't, donations have been coming in now that the word is getting out that we're here for all kids."

"Is that primarily Pastor Jeff's doing?" She smiled as Beth dipped one delicate toe in the water. A second later she plunged in, shrieking with delight. Because Tanner didn't answer she turned to glance at him, found him watching her. "Tanner?"

"Partly Jeff's. That street mission work he's

doing gives him a lot of contacts with kids who need help. I'm glad he asked me to partner with him on that." He shrugged, then chewed on a stem of grass for a moment. "It's also due in part to Rod and Trent. I guess they talk up Wranglers Ranch quite a bit."

"No wonder. You've been great with them," she praised. "Does that mean you aren't worried about Tige anymore?"

"Not exactly. I don't want him to come here, if that's what you're asking." Why didn't he look at her?

"It isn't." Sophie frowned. "A few weeks ago you were seriously worried about him, though I'm still not clear exactly why. Did he threaten you or something?"

"Tige doesn't threaten."

"Well, something about him bothered you enough to hire that security outfit that now keeps watch on Wranglers." Confused and uncertain, Sophie waited for an explanation. "Yet today you seem almost nonchalant."

"I'm not nonchalant." Tanner's voice tightened. "The security guys haven't seen or heard anything and there haven't been any other incidents. Since kids are coming here, which is what I wanted, I'm trying to focus on what I'm here to do and leave Tige up to God."

"Yes, but—" Nervous about her burgeoning

feelings for Tanner but hesitant to reveal them when he seemed to be distancing himself, Sophie finally asked the question that had been plaguing her. "Did you have a girlfriend when you lived on the streets?"

Tanner's head jerked toward her. His face tightened into a mask Sophie had seen only once before, for a few moments the morning after the fire.

"Why do you ask that?" he growled.

"Because you never talk about your past. I've told you all kinds of things about Marty and my past life," Sophie snapped, irritated that this sense of foreboding still troubled her. "But I know almost nothing about yours."

"There's nothing to know." Tanner smiled at her, but it wasn't his usual open smile. This one hid shadows in the back of his rich green eyes. The ball Davy and Beth had been throwing rolled toward him. As if relieved, he jumped to his feet to retrieve it. "I'm going to throw them a few," he said and walked away.

Sophie was about to nod but since he wasn't looking at her she clamped her lips shut, frustrated by the barrier that had seemed to come between them. Tanner laughed and joked with her children while she sat stewing about his attitude and lack of forthrightness. She yearned to be part of the fun the others were having but she couldn't settle. She wanted to trust Tanner was everything he seemed to be.

But what if she trusted him and he betrayed her?

Questions about Tanner and his past tormented Sophie until finally she rose and walked toward a gray-barked sycamore tree near their horses. She admired the beautifully arched white branches loaded with large star-shaped leaves before lifting down the knapsack she'd packed earlier. She took out a thermos of coffee and poured herself a cup.

And froze.

There on the ground, where Tanner had been sitting just a minute earlier, lay a picture. Sophie bent, picked it up and swallowed hard. It was a copy of an ultrasound picture of an unborn child.

*Tanner's child?*

Her knees buckled at the thought. Clutching her coffee, she sank onto a sun-warmed rock, unable to get past that thought. She sipped her black coffee, willing her hands to move, her brain to work, her thoughts to organize.

Sophie had no idea how much time had passed when she heard the kids' voices coming closer. Without even thinking she slipped the picture into the pocket of her capris not knowing why, only aware that she needed time to make sense of her suddenly tilting world.

"We're ready for a snack," Tanner said, his usual tone in place. Then he frowned at her. "Sophie?"

"Yes. A snack." She dredged up a smile while suppressing the urge to scream *traitor*. After all, she didn't know anything about this picture yet. "Good thing I packed some cookies."

"Are you all right?" His voice couldn't have been more caring nor could the hand he placed on her shoulder have been more tender. "Don't you feel well?"

"Actually I don't. I think I'll sit here and relax with my coffee while you guys have your snack." She returned to her former seat, away from his touch, his voice and those all-seeing eyes. "I'll be fine," she assured him when he kept watching her.

Of course she would be. She had to be.

Because if there was one lesson Sophie had learned it was self-reliance. But while she maintained her stoic face, her heart cried,

*Whom do I trust now, God?*

"There's something wrong so you might as well tell me what it is." Tanner sat on Sophie's lumpy sofa and waited for the ax to fall. "The kids are in bed, probably sleeping, and you don't have a job scheduled for tomorrow so you have no excuse to keep you from telling me what it is."

Sophie said nothing, simply reached into her

pocket and slid something out. She set it on the coffee table in front of him. "You dropped this when we were at the creek."

Tanner knew she wouldn't ask him about the photo. She wanted to. He could see the questions filling her dark eyes. But she'd asked him about his past so often and he'd always rebuffed her. He knew she wouldn't ask again.

Explaining was the very last thing he wanted to do. But for ages he'd been telling her to trust. Now it was his turn to trust her—with the truth.

"The picture is of my son. He died before he was ever born."

Sophie caught her breath but gave no other visible sign that she was affected.

"I have to start at the beginning, okay?" When she nodded, he sighed. "Remember the friend I asked you about, the one who walked away from his pregnant girlfriend?" Her eyes flared and he nodded. "It was me. Her name was Amy and the day Burt invited me to live with him she'd just told me she was pregnant."

"But how— When…?" Sophie's lips pinched together. She sat back and waited.

"I know what I did was wrong. I know I should have taken care of her, at least made sure she was all right. I had a responsibility and I dodged it, ran away to a world I'd only ever dreamed about." Tanner could tell by her expression that Sophie was horrified. "I should have been there for Amy and I wasn't. I will always be ashamed of that."

"Why did you do it?" she whispered.

"I don't know if you can understand how unbelievable Burt's offer was to me." Even now Tanner was amazed that he of all people had been selected to live at Wranglers. "I'd been on the street for three months. I was scared, hungry, alone and going nowhere fast. I knew that if I stayed on the streets it wouldn't be long before Tige would convince me to start using. I knew I'd end up exactly like him if I did."

"Burt?"

"He said I'd have a home. I'd never had that, Sophie. Not a home of my own. He said I wouldn't be hungry, that he'd teach me how to work with horses. I was a mess with people," he joked but found no corresponding mirth on her face. "But I got along real good with his horses. Maybe because we both just want someone to love us." Admitting that was embarrassing.

"I see." Sophie frowned. "What did Burt say about Amy?"

"I didn't tell him." Tanner hung his head. "I didn't think—no, I *knew* he wouldn't let me go with him if he knew about her and the baby. He'd been taking me out for lunch, to church, to the ranch—stuff I'd only ever dreamed of. He had a house, a place where he could be his own boss, and I knew from his church talk that he would never beat me."

"So you accepted." She said it as if she'd expected nothing more.

"No. I refused at first. But when I told Amy she told me to go. She was in love with another guy by then. She didn't want anything to do with me anymore. I figured it was the same old, same old. Nobody cared what Tanner Johns did." He studied her, praying, hoping she could understand his desperation.

But all Sophie said was "Go on," in that crisp, cool voice that was not the real Sophie, not the woman he'd come to care about.

"So I thought why not take what Burt was offering. Nobody would care. I could finish school and most of all, I could get away from Tige. So I gave Amy every cent I had, all two hundred dollars." He smiled, remembering how massive that sum had seemed. "And I walked away, all the way to Wranglers Ranch. And I'm still here."

"But—didn't it bother you?" Sophie wanted to know.

"Every day and every night," Tanner told her honestly. "I'd think about that baby, wonder when his birthday was, if he could walk or talk, what color his eyes were, if he was all right. I was desperate to know about my child. So one day I went back to find out." He stopped, the memory still powerful enough to catch his breath.

"And?"

"Tige told me Amy was gone. That's when I knew I'd lost any chance I ever had to have the family I'd always wanted." Tanner sat in silent shame.

He wasn't going to tell her that Tige had beaten him within an inch of his life because he wouldn't sell his drugs. He wasn't going to mention that he'd lain in pain under a sheet of cardboard for two days, until Burt had found him and taken him to the hospital. He sure wasn't going to tell her how hard it now was to keep going back to those awful streets, to keep some other kid from being as stupid as he'd been.

"I'm sorry, Tanner. No wonder you didn't want to talk about it," Sophie said in a very quiet voice.

"I'd talk about it nonstop if it meant he could have lived." He rose and picked up the picture, let his forefinger trail over the face he now loved. "It should have been me who died. I deserved it. Not him."

"I'm so sorry, Tanner." Her hand touched his shoulder in the briefest caress.

Tanner turned into her arms, desperate to find—what? Solace? Forgiveness? Love?

Sophie hesitated, patted his shoulder and then when he would have drawn her close, eased free and moved four feet away.

"I'm truly sorry, Tanner. But I'm glad you

told me. You needed to tell someone, to let out the pain."

"I guess." He slid the picture into his pocket without taking his gaze from her. His heart sank. Sophie looked as if she was waiting. For him to leave?

As he studied her stiff figure he knew immediately that whatever she'd felt, or whatever he'd hoped she'd feel, was now gone. Sophie didn't trust easily. In her eyes, by leaving Amy, he'd betrayed in the worst possible way.

"I'd better go. See you soon?" He hoped.

"I'll be busy for the next few weeks," she said quickly. Too quickly. "But I'm catering your Independence Day celebration, remember? I think the kids are really looking forward to it."

"Yeah." So now they were employer and employee? "Sophie—"

"I'm really tired, Tanner. I'd like to get some rest. But thank you for today."

"Yeah. Sure." He walked to the door, took his hat off the hook and glanced around one last time. Something inside him died as he realized he wouldn't be coming back here again. Sophie didn't want a man she couldn't trust in her life.

Now she stood holding the door open, waiting to escort him out of her world.

Tanner walked forward. But he stopped on the threshold and, without pausing to think, did the only thing he could. He leaned forward and kissed Sophie Armstrong the way he'd always wanted to.

And to his utter amazement and joy, Sophie kissed him back the way he wanted to be kissed, as if he was precious, wanted. It was as if something stronger than either of them pushed them to break through the barriers they'd put up to protect their inner selves.

Against what? Against this powerful, heartrending certainty that no one could ever mean so much?

Tanner's arms tightened around the woman whose smile could make his day. Feeling Sophie's heart beat against his answered every question about what was important in his life. He'd never been happier than he was right now.

But Sophie wasn't his. By withholding the truth he'd lost her trust.

With regret dragging at him he loosed his arms and stepped back. He smoothed the tears from her cheeks, brushed her shiny brown hair from her eyes and traced her wonderful lips with one lingering caress.

"Goodbye, Sophie."

Then Tanner walked out the door to a future guaranteed to be the same as his past.

Alone.

# Chapter Eleven

"Why doesn't Mr. Cowboy come here anymore, Mama?"

Sophie had been waiting for the question. Truthfully she hadn't expected Beth to wait more than a month before asking.

"Yeah," Davy chimed in. "How come we don't go to Wranglers Ranch anymore?"

"You still go, Davy," Sophie reminded him. "You work there two days a week."

"But that's work. School's been out for ages but I don't get to do fun things with Tanner anymore," her son protested.

"Tanner's busy. He has camps going for other kids. He doesn't have time to play with you." She pressed toothpicks with little flags on top into each cupcake. "Anyway, we are going to Wranglers today."

"Just to deliver food. Then you'll make up an

excuse why we have to leave. Again." Davy's glowering face said he understood exactly what she was doing.

"I like Mr. Cowboy," Beth said quietly, favoring her mother with an intense stare.

"So do I." *Way too much for my own good.* "And for your information we're going to be at Wranglers Ranch until late tonight." Suppressing the bubble of joy inside her that matched her children's grins, Sophie said, "We're going to leave in twenty minutes. Please straighten your rooms and make your beds before we leave."

"Why? Who's going to see them?" Davy grumbled, pushing away from the breakfast table. "Nobody ever comes to this boring place."

"Boring," Beth added before she scooted off to her room.

Sophie couldn't argue with the truth. Without Tanner life *was* dull. But that was the way it had to be. She'd made that decision after he'd told her about his unborn child. Though it had been painfully clear that Tanner regretted his actions and though Sophie accepted that he'd been very young to make such a momentous decision, she'd realized that she didn't really know Tanner enough to trust him. Even now she couldn't get past her disappointment in his selfish actions. As she'd listened to his explanations with her heart aching for his loss, she'd accepted that he deeply mourned losing the son he clearly now longed for.

But accompanied by her empathy was the memory of her own suffering as a single mom, alone, desperate, terrified she'd fail her kids because Marty hadn't provided for them. His selfish decisions had cost her dearly. Still did. Even though Wranglers had boosted her income, even though Tanner had touted her skills so that she could now pick and choose jobs, Sophie still worried. What if, God forbid, something happened to her?

Sophie couldn't afford to love Tanner, though that didn't stop her heart from wanting his arms around her, or end her yearning for him to kiss her as he had. So she'd distanced herself by being brisk and businesslike and avoiding any chance of intimacy between them. Apparently Tanner felt the same because though he was always unfailingly polite and welcoming when she had a job at Wranglers or when she saw them at church, he no longer came to her house, teased her or made those affectionate gestures she'd come to cherish.

Sophie had contemplated walking away from her commitments to Wranglers and Tanner. But she couldn't do it, and not just because she'd spent the deposit he'd given her for Wranglers' Fourth of July party. Davy adored the skateboard she'd bought for his birthday, and the new stove in her kitchen was a necessity. But the real reason she hadn't canceled was because she couldn't bear to disappoint Tanner. Because he'd been disappointed too many times already. No matter how hard she tried to be cool and calculating, Sophie couldn't get rid of the strong love she felt for the rancher.

She was mad at God for that. How could He have let her fall for the wrong man again, and not just the wrong man but one her children adored? God had let their lives become intertwined with the ranch so much that this break with Tanner was causing her kids pain. That was the last thing she wanted and it only reinforced her feelings of distrust.

So Sophie slowly distanced herself from Wranglers, hoping Beth and Davy would find other things to fill their world. Clearly that wasn't working. Why oh why had God let this happen?

Stuffing down her yearning for things to go back the way they were, Sophie mocked herself. Pretending Tanner hadn't abandoned his girlfriend, and being with a man she couldn't trust was not the answer. Self-sufficiency was.

With a sigh for the trust that still eluded her, Sophie packed up the containers she'd filled with lunch goodies for the church-sponsored trail ride at Wranglers and tonight's barbecue, loaded the kids and drove to her job site. She would keep her word, provide food for today's party as she'd agreed. But once her Fourth of July commitment was complete, Sophie wasn't going back to Wranglers. Better to make a clean break. Davy and Beth would just have to deal with it.

"Hello, Mrs. Armstrong." The security guard nodded at the kids and waved her through onto Wranglers Ranch. That interaction combined with the sight of a new metal gate closing as she drove to the house gave Sophie a moment of anxiety, but she brushed it away. It had been weeks now and Tige hadn't made an appearance. Tanner was simply being cautious.

"Hey, Sophie. How are you?" The object of her thoughts opened her van door.

"I'm fine." Tanner looked gaunt, she thought. As if he wasn't sleeping well. Because of her? A trickle of guilt filtered through her but she ignored it and handed Beth and Davy items to carry inside.

"We'll have a hungry bunch of cowpokes today," Tanner said. He took the largest bin from her and indicated she should pile another on it.

"I have plenty of food," she told him, walking into the kitchen and hoping he wouldn't linger. Having him so near made her want things that could not be.

"And extra?" he asked quietly. "Tige's kids showed up with some friends."

"There will be enough for everyone." She glanced out the window. "The ranch looks very busy."

"It is." Tanner frowned. "We have so many coming every day. The day camps aren't enough. Originally I'd planned to build cabins so we could do overnighters but…" He leaned back on his heels without finishing his sentence.

"But?" she prodded. "That's not possible now?" she asked after nodding permission for Davy and Beth to go check on the rabbits.

"It's possible," he said quietly. "I'm just not sure how to go about it. I'm no builder."

"Can't you hire someone?" Sophie mixed the lemonade and added ice from his fridge.

"If I could find an architect with the right vision." He met her gaze and shrugged. "I want a certain type of cabin that doesn't look out of place."

"I'm sorry," she murmured sympathetically while keeping her head averted, hoping, no, praying he would leave.

"Sophie, is everything okay?" There was a hesitancy to Tanner's question that told her he felt the chill she was sending his way.

"The food will be prepared and served as you requested." She couldn't help the stiffness in her voice. Hadn't she come through often enough for

Tanner that he should know better than to question her? Why didn't he trust her?

*As you trust him?*

"Just checking." His slow, lazy smile reappeared for an instant, then dissolved when she didn't return it. "I'll leave you to it, then. Let me know if you need anything."

"Uh-huh." Sophie watched him go. If only... "Tanner?"

"Yes?" His green eyes lit up and his whole body language showed expectancy. Of what? Did he think she'd change her mind?

"Tige?" The light in his eyes died.

"Haven't heard from him." He clamped his Stetson on his head and walked to the door. "See you later."

Not if she could avoid it, Sophie thought, watching him stride across the yard with a longing she couldn't suppress. *Why did You let me love him, God?* her heart wept.

*Trust in the Lord with all your heart and lean not unto your own understanding. In all your ways acknowledge Him and He will direct your paths.*

Trust. It always came down to that. And, as usual, she couldn't do that. Couldn't trust Tanner. Couldn't trust God.

*I'm scared to,* she admitted silently. *Help me?*

"Sophie?" Monica studied her with a perplexed look. "I asked if you wanted Tiffany and me to start buttering buns."

"Yes, please," Sophie said in an effort to pretend everything was normal, which it so was not. Nothing had been normal since the day she'd met Tanner. And probably wouldn't be again unless she could get rid of this overpowering love for him. "I'm glad you're here early, girls. It's going to be a busy day. Happy Fourth of July."

*Now get to work, Sophie, and forget Tanner Johns.*

"Nice work with the decor, Moses." Tanner admired the array of banners and flags that decorated the ranch. "Wranglers is looking mighty festive."

"Thanks." The old man didn't look at him as he dug a stone out of Abishag's shoe. "We've got two lame horses but the others are good to go."

"We're going to need every one. The place is crawling with kids just waiting to get on a horse. Where's Lefty?" Tanner asked after he'd found nothing among their tack that needed repair.

"He and Bo took some beginners out for a short trial ride to test their skills. They'll be back in five." Moses's frown told Tanner he had something on his mind. "I been praying about those boys, Trent and the other one."

"Rod," Tanner supplied. "Why? Something wrong?"

"Don't rightly know," Moses admitted, scratching his head. "They seemed real worried when they were here yesterday. The bigger kid had a mess of bruises on his arm."

Tanner forced down a rush of anger. "It happens" was all he said.

"Yeah. Too often." Moses frowned. "They said they needed to tell you something but you were on that ride and they couldn't wait."

"I'll talk to them today, if they show up," Tanner promised.

"You talk to Sophie?" Moses lifted one bushy brow when Tanner frowned at him.

"About what?"

"Dunno," the old man said somberly. "Just seems to me you two got some sorting out to do like maybe that girl you walked out on before you came here." Moses patted Abishag's side. "The one who was going to have your baby?"

Tanner gaped. "You knew?"

"'Course." Moses nodded. "Burt told me."

"Burt?" His face burned with shame. "I never told him about Amy or the baby."

"Didn't need to. Burt had a way of findin' things out." Moses smiled. "Smart old coot, that man. Kinda like me." He wheezed a laugh at Tanner's surprised face. "Burt an' me only look gullible, son."

"Yes, but—" Tanner couldn't get it to sink in. "Burt knew everything?"

"Pretty much. He found the girl, gave her some

money and kept sending more every month after her new boyfriend dumped her." Moses stared off into the distance. "Even paid for a grave and a marker when your baby died so as you'd be able to mourn proper. Guess he forgot to tell you that part, but ol' Burt sure did love you, Tanner."

The private investigator he'd hired had said nothing about a grave. "I wish Burt had told me," he muttered.

"Reckon he was waiting for you to speak first." Moses slapped on his hat. "Wouldn't have made any difference anyway, would it?"

"Yes." Tanner unclenched his tense. "If I'd known where Amy was I might have apologized to her, tried to make it up to her or something." He met Moses's stare. "I should never have let her go like that knowing she was pregnant with my child."

"No," Moses agreed. "That wasn't right. I'm guessing your lady knows?" He lifted one of his bushy brows.

Tanner nodded and explained about the investigator he'd hired.

"Somehow he got hold a copy of the baby's ultrasound from the hospital. I dropped it and Sophie found it. I had to tell her the truth when she asked," he muttered, embarrassed and yet relieved to tell Moses. "After hearing that, Sophie changed. She thinks she can't trust me, that I'd leave her and the kids vulnerable."

"Would you?" Moses studied Tanner with narrowed eyes.

"Never. I love Sophie. This past month has been agony. To see her yet feel that icy barrier between us—" Tanner squeezed his eyes closed against the pain. "She avoids me, makes excuses not to come here or sneaks away when I am."

"I know," Moses said. "Her boy told me she's not happy."

"Maybe that's why I can't make more headway with my plans for Wranglers. Maybe God can't use somebody who's messed up as much as I have." He stared at his dusty boots. "I always wanted a family, you know that. But that's not going to happen because I've made too many mistakes. I probably wouldn't make a good father anyway."

"Hogwash! Burt wouldn't have let it pass so neither will I," Moses chided. "God forgives. That's the very basis of our faith. We're human. We mess up. And God forgives."

"Yes." Tanner thought it through, then nodded. "But even so, I'm not doing what Burt wanted with this place. He had a heart for street kids and we haven't focused on only them. I can't make Wranglers into the kind of camp he envisioned."

"Burt was the best friend I ever had but he

wasn't God. You gotta focus on figuring out what *God* wants you to do," Moses insisted. "Burt would have told you that God's your boss so you do what He's telling you to do."

"I'm not sure I know how," he admitted.

"You do, boy." Moses sounded just as stubborn as he had the day Tanner said he couldn't learn to ride. "The good Lord gave you talents to do what He needs done."

"We're back to that verse again, huh?" Tanner sighed. "The 'fan your gift into flame' one? But I don't have a gift, Moses. I'm just a plain ordinary cowboy."

"Ain't no such thing, son," Moses said in a dry mocking tone. "But you surely have been gifted."

"With what?" Tanner demanded. "And how do you and Sophie know when I don't?"

"Always thought she was a smart lady." Moses slapped him on the shoulder. "Don't you get it? You have the gift of leadership. Burt watched how the hands just naturally turned to you. They saw you as their leader when he wasn't there. After Burt died they knew they could count on you to keep the place rolling, to keep their jobs. You have a knack for getting folks to work together and that helps them give their best. Never knew anybody as good at getting folks to pitch in. Folks like that nice lady and her kids."

"Sophie won't be coming around to help much anymore," Tanner assured him gloomily.

"God told you that, did He?" Moses sniffed. "Don't matter what you think. God's got His reasons for bringing her here. He's got it all planned out."

"So what am I supposed to do?" Frustration made his voice sharp. "Hang around when I'm not wanted?"

"You be there in case she needs you." Moses glared at him. "You love this woman and her kids? Or are you scared of loving somebody like her, somebody who wants more from a man than just words? She doesn't need some guy who won't stick by her. She's got two kids to raise. You up for that?"

"Yes! I love her," Tanner almost yelled, irritated by Moses's pushing.

"Then prove it. Be there for her. Let God work out the rest." Moses grinned. "He brought you together. He can figure the rest out, too."

Tanner swallowed, humbled by the old man's faith. Moses trusted God. Tanner needed to do the same.

"Here comes Lefty. I gotta go help him." Moses leaned over to peer into Tanner's face. "Didn't upset you, did I, son?"

"I'll survive—"

"Mr. Cowboy!" Beth's voice echoed in the warm air.

"Since you think leadership is my gift, guess I better get on with directing this show." He couldn't quite believe that. Not yet anyway. "Thanks, Moses."

"You bet. Just keep your eyes on God and remember, Burt didn't choose no dummy." Cackling with laughter, Moses shuffled away.

Tanner forced the door of his brain to close on the thousands of questions that rippled through his head so he could deal with Beth's escaped rabbits.

*I don't know if all Moses said was true*, he prayed as he worked. *But I know I haven't trusted You enough. So I'm leaving Sophie and our relationship up to You. Please help her learn to trust me.*

Having turned over the woman he loved to the One who loved her even more than he did, and because he couldn't stay away, Tanner walked purposefully toward the kitchen with Beth to find out if the cook needed his help.

From now on Sophie Armstrong was going to find it hard to get rid of this cowboy.

## Chapter Twelve

With the Independence Day party in full swing, Sophie hated to take a midafternoon break but she couldn't argue with the boss, especially when he was sitting on the bench right next to her.

"I meant to tell you." Desperate to distance herself, Sophie inched away from Tanner's big body. "Edna said to thank you for the flowers and for fixing her leaky faucet last week." She pinned him with her severest gaze. "Apparently you also helped Davy fix our coffee table and re-paste the living room wallpaper."

"Edna and I were having coffee while she was watching your kids and Davy mentioned there were issues so…" He shrugged as if the chores were inconsequential. "No biggie."

"Well, thank you from her and from us." She hesitated to continue, to end things between them.

"Thanks but don't come around anymore?"

Tanner chuckled at her expression. "I know you'd prefer that, Sophie. You've found me wanting in the responsibility department. And you should. I made a bad mistake ten years ago."

"Tanner—"

"But that was ten years ago," he reminded quietly. "I'm not that dumb kid anymore. I've changed and I intend to prove it to you. You're not going to get rid of me." He leaned closer and covered her hand with his. "I love you, Sophie. I'm sorry if that isn't what you want to hear but it's the truth and I'll keep saying it until you start to trust me."

"I don't know if that's ever going to happen—"

"Sophie, we're out of lemonade." Tiffany waited for instruction.

Frustrated by her interruption at this most inopportune moment, Sophie rose, desperate to make Tanner understand that she wasn't going to change her mind and that he couldn't keep hanging around, waiting for that. It couldn't happen because having Tanner near made Sophie want things she couldn't have. She huffed a sigh of resignation and went to deal with the issue.

More kids arrived as afternoon turned to evening and each time Sophie needed something it seemed Tanner was there just in time to lend a hand, offer a suggestion or simply encourage her with generous praise. But by the time her barbecue supper was over Sophie began to lag. Somehow Tanner noticed that, too, and insisted she sit down with Davy and Beth, who'd been having a ball, Beth in the bouncy castle and Davy running errands for the hands who were kept busy with would-be riders.

"It's a really fun party, Tanner," Davy enthused. "I sure like making Moses's campfire pies."

Sophie made a face. All the food she'd prepared and her son preferred two slices of white bread with canned pie filling, cooked in a metal tin over the fire!

"I like these cookies your mother made." Tanner deliberately bumped his shoulder against hers, smiled when she drew away and crunched on his third cookie.

His smile warmed Sophie from the top of her head to the tips of her toes and finished in a warm fuzzy glow that made her want to snuggle against his side. Why did she care for him so much? She didn't want to, didn't want to risk what caring could mean—risking her security to trust in a guy who'd already proved untrustworthy seemed foolish in the extreme.

And so wonderfully alluring.

"What do you like best, Beth?" Tanner asked.

"I like people to be happy." Beth studied him. "Do you think this is what heaven is like, Mr. Cowboy?"

"Like Wranglers Ranch?" Seeing she was utterly serious, Tanner smothered his laughter. "Maybe."

"I like it when people are happy," she said with a frown. "I don't like arguing and fighting."

"Did you see someone fighting, Beth?" Sophie saw Tanner's immediate alertness. "Or arguing?" he added.

"Uh-huh." Her daughter's blue eyes darkened. Sophie was about to ask what troubled Beth when Tanner touched her arm and gave the slightest shake of his head. So she left it to him to probe further.

"Can you tell me about it?" His voice was so gentle.

"I didn't hear very much," Beth said. Sophie's concern escalated when her daughter glanced over one shoulder worriedly.

"It's okay, sweetheart," Tanner said in a very tender voice. "Just tell me what you did hear."

After studying him for a moment, Beth finally whispered, "It wasn't a nice voice."

"Was it a man speaking?" Tanner asked. Beth nodded. "What did he say?"

"Today's the day." She waited, her blue gaze riveted on Tanner.

"But sweetie, that's not fighting or arguing," Sophie chided.

"That was the other voice."

"What did it say?" Davy wanted to know.

Beth bit her lip. She looked to Sophie for reassurance. Sophie nodded and squeezed her hand.

"Tanner can't help unless you tell him, Bethy."

"He said, 'Tanner won't like it. You'll have to hurt him.'" Her voice cracked. "Are you gonna get hurt, Mr. Cowboy?" Tears spilled down her cheeks. "I don't want you to be hurt. I love you."

"I love you, too, Beth." Tanner lifted Beth onto his knee and hugged her in his strong, capable arms.

Sophie gulped, blinking away the rush of her own tears. Seeing the big tough rancher comfort her troubled, confused daughter brought a swell of love for him that she was helpless to stop. Again the questions rolled through her brain.

What if she trusted him with her love? Tanner had stuck with her, pitching in when he didn't have to. He'd taken care of her kids as well as any father could. Other than not telling her about his past he'd been totally up-front and a lot more than a good friend. What if she let herself accept everything he was offering her? What if she took a chance that Tanner Johns loved her enough to stick by her, no matter what?

*What if she was wrong?*

"You don't have to be afraid, Bethy," he said lovingly, brushing away her bangs to press a kiss against her forehead. "We have God caring for us, remember? Can you think of a verse that says that? How about, 'If God be for us, who can be against us?'"

"I have one, too." With the shadows chased away, Beth's blue eyes shone. "'Therefore I will not fear.'"

"That's a very good verse to remember, Beth." Tanner hugged her but his eyes narrowed as they met Sophie's. "Let's pray and ask God to keep everyone safe and happy today." He bowed his head and offered a short prayer that all visitors to the ranch today would learn more about God. Then he gazed at her, his green eyes filled with tenderness. "And God, help us learn to trust."

Sophie's face burned with shame. Why couldn't she trust him? Everyone else seemed to. Thankfully Tanner didn't seem to notice her embarrassment since Lefty walked over and murmured something in his ear. Sophie heard the word *security* but little else. Then Lefty, grim-faced, stepped back.

"Okay, kids. When do you think we should cut that massive red, white and blue cake your mother ma—"

"Well, well. Isn't this a special family gathering? Hello, Tanner old buddy."

Tige. Sophie knew it immediately and cringed. Beside her, Beth snuggled against her and whispered, "Therefore I will not fear."

"Hey, Tige. Welcome here." Other than a slight narrowing of his eyes, Tanner showed no visible sign that he was annoyed by the man's arrival as he shook hands. "Glad you could come." His voice tightened a fraction when he said, "Hello, Amy."

*Amy? As in Amy the mother of Tanner's son?* Sophie's stomach dropped as fear took hold.

"Tanner." An apologetic look washed over Amy's thin, pale face. "I didn't want to come—"

"Why not? Everyone is invited to Wranglers Ranch's Fourth of July party, right, Tanner?" A cunning look filled Tige's golden eyes. "'Least that's what *my* sons told me."

The emphasis wasn't lost on Sophie and she'd doubted Tanner had missed it, either.

"Your sons are right." Tanner seemed nonchalant. "You're welcome here, Amy." He smiled warmly. "This is Sophie and her children, Beth and Davy."

"Nice to meet you," Sophie replied automatically in as friendly a tone as she could manage, taking her cue from Tanner.

"You, too," Amy said halfheartedly, barely glancing at her.

"Lulu sends her regrets. She's, uh, indisposed." Tige cackled, an evil sound that made Sophie shiver.

"I'm sorry to hear that. Would you like something to eat? Sophie's an excellent cook." Tanner didn't rise to the bait when Tige asked for whiskey. "Sorry. This is a ranch for kids. We don't keep alcohol here."

Lefty stood nearby watching so Tanner asked him to bring Tige and Amy coffee.

"The boys say this little lady makes some good pie. I could use a piece of that," Tige muttered after he'd taken a sip of black coffee.

"We don't have pie today but I made a big Independence Day cake," Sophie offered. "Want some of that?"

"Sure." Tige studied her. "So you're Tanner's new Amy."

"No, I'm the cook at Wranglers Ranch," Sophie said evenly. "Would you like to see the kitchen?" She aimed her question at Amy, who nodded eagerly.

"I've got some jobs for these guys." Lefty beckoned to Beth and Davy. He shot a look at Tanner, who gave a barely perceptible nod. "Come on, guys."

Clearly they'd worked this out beforehand. Sophie felt a rush of pure love for the big rancher's forethought in protecting her kids. She wanted them far away from Tige. She led Amy into the house.

"It's a wonderful kitchen to work in—" Sophie paused when Amy laid a hand on her arm.

"I'm sorry we butted in," she said quietly. "I only agreed to come because I owe Tanner an apology about the baby." She paused, frowned. "You know about that?"

Sophie nodded.

"I took off back then because I knew Tanner would have made me quit using and in those days all I wanted was my next fix," Amy admitted shamefacedly.

"I see."

"Tanner was always trying to help. He's the only guy I ever knew who stood up to Tige. I'm glad he got out." She waved a hand. "This place, this ranch, it suits him. My husband says Tanner's place is making a big difference to the city's youth."

"You're married?" Sophie said, surprised.

"To a cop. Can you believe it?" Amy laughed. "My husband suggested I agree to come with Tige. He said it was time I told Tanner the truth about the baby. But I think he already knows." She frowned. "Anyway after Tanner left with the old man, Tige said he came back to look for me." She frowned. "You knew that, too? Bet you didn't know Tige beat him so badly he almost killed him. Well, he did. You see, Tige was furious. He had lost control of Tanner and he didn't like that. Anyway I'd told Tanner I loved somebody else and that I was going away with him. And Tanner, being Tanner, gave me every dime he owned and wished me the best."

"But he should have helped you," Sophie protested. "He shouldn't have just walked away and left you to manage."

"It wasn't Tanner who left, Sophie. It was me. And with Tige's help I made sure he couldn't find me when that conscience of his took over." Amy shook her head. "To this day I don't know how God can love somebody as mixed up as I was. For a while I didn't believe He did. I guess I should explain."

"You don't have to," Sophie murmured.

"It would help, though, wouldn't it?" Amy nodded. "Because you're in love with him."

"I—"

"Tanner's one of those guys who deserves love. I wish I'd loved him back then but I couldn't even love myself."

"You weren't in love with Tanner?" Surprised, Sophie watched regret fill her face.

"I wish I had. But Tanner was only ever a safe place for me, a refuge from Tige's and Lulu's rages. That's why I latched on to him. I never once thought about what Tanner needed," she admitted. "Falling in love with my husband taught me that love isn't about yourself. It's all about the one you love, protecting them, trusting them.

Even now I still struggle with trusting that Jack only wants what's best for me."

"How did you learn to trust?" Achingly aware that she craved this woman's confidence in Tanner's trustworthiness, Sophie paid attention.

"Ever seen that demonstration where a person closes his eyes and lets himself fall backward, trusting his loved ones to catch him?" Amy chuckled at Sophie's dark look. "Sounds horrifying, doesn't it? But that's kind of what you have to do. You can't have a relationship if you're always waiting for the other person to fail you. Because they will. Humans fail. If you put your trust in God, though, He never fails."

"Telling secrets, Amy?" Tige leaned in the doorway.

"Actually we were talking about her husband." Sophie stared at the bleary-eyed man, despising the smug look in his eyes. "Sounds like he's one of the good guys. Like Tanner." She wanted to escape Tige. "Since you're here at Wranglers Ranch maybe you'd like to go for a short trail ride, Amy? Or there's a walkabout trail."

"Trail ride sounds good. Would you show me where to go?"

Sophie was about to point until she realized the other woman had something else to say.

"I'll show you the way." She led Amy outside.

When they were no longer visible from the house, Amy stopped her.

"This is far enough, thanks. That's my husband over there standing by the tree. The big guy with the green shirt," Amy said, love filling her voice. "He wouldn't let me come without him and now he's taking me home but I wanted to warn you first."

"Warn me?" A tickle of breeze made Sophie shiver though the evening was warm. "About what?"

"Lulu is here somewhere, and she and Tige are planning something." Amy's eyes darkened. "I don't know what but I know it isn't good. Tige has always resented that Tanner got off the streets, that he never got hooked, that Tige couldn't control him." Her lips tightened. "When Tige found out that his sons have been coming here, he was furious. He thinks Tanner is trying to take them away from him. Be very careful. Tige's dangerous and when he needs a fix he'll do anything to get it. He needs one now." She squeezed Sophie's hand. "Take care of Tanner, okay? You'll never meet a man you can trust more."

This from the woman whom Tanner had abandoned? Or had he?

Sophie was no longer so sure.

"I have to go."

A moment later Amy and her husband blended

into the crowd, then disappeared, leaving Sophie bewildered and confused. She walked slowly, thinking about what Amy had said. After ensuring the kids were still safe with Lefty at the barn, Sophie was about to slip into the kitchen when she heard Tige's voice.

"So this place is all yours?"

"Burt, the owner, wanted the ranch turned into a kids' camp." Sophie could hear Tanner's hesitation and knew he didn't want to reveal too much.

"But you're in charge, right?" Tige pressed. "You're the boss here?"

"I guess." Sophie had a clear mental image of Tanner shrugging, as if being in charge meant little.

"Man, a place like this must be worth a fortune."

When Tanner didn't respond Sophie stepped around the corner to rescue him.

"Oh, you're still here, Tanner. Good. Can you help me in the kitchen, please?"

"Sure." He rose to his lanky height. "You hanging around for the fireworks, Tige?"

"Me, I love fireworks. Of course I'm staying," he said in a sly tone. The noise Tige made was not a laugh. "Hey, where's Amy?" he asked, suddenly sobering.

"Oh, she wanted to try her hand at our dart

game," Sophie said breezily. "Maybe you would, too. There's a nice prize for the winner."

"Is there, now? A nice prize." Tige began to walk away but then paused to toss a "See you later, Tanner" over one shoulder. He grinned, his half-rotten teeth giving him a ghoulish look. "You can count on that, buddy. You owe me and I always collect on my debts."

As Tige walked away, laughing crazily, Sophie watched Tanner. She blinked when the handsome cowboy suddenly drew her into the shadows, into his arms and held her fast.

"Tanner, what are you—"

She couldn't say another word because Tanner Johns was kissing her as if she was the only thing that mattered in his world. And there under the whispering mesquite trees, Sophie kissed him back because she couldn't help herself.

She loved Tanner Johns.

# Chapter Thirteen

"Oh, Sophie. I was so scared Tige would try something. I couldn't bear for you to be hurt because of me."

Tanner bent his head, unable to stop himself from embracing the woman who filled his world with joy, reveling in the way her lips responded to his, taking and giving. This woman, this special woman, was so dear. He couldn't help but reveal his deepest longing—to have her stay in his world as she'd stayed in his heart for so long.

"I love you, Sophie. I love you so much."

He bent his head to tell her without using more words how much she meant to him. To his delight her arms lifted and slid around his neck and she kissed him back with so much passion his heart sang with joy. When she finally drew away to catch her breath, he lovingly traced the delicate curve of her jaw, the graceful arch of her neck, only to home in once more on her lips.

"I love you, Sophie."

And then the dream ended.

Sophie pulled free of his embrace. "I'm sorry, but I can't love you, Tanner."

"Can't or won't?" he demanded. "After all this time, after everything we've shared, you're still afraid to trust me?"

Her nod killed every hope he'd clung to. He turned away, unable to stand there and let her feel sorry for him. He wanted her love, not her pity.

"Where are you going?" she asked softly.

"I'm hosting a party, remember?" But Tanner paused because he knew his Sophie and right now she had something to say.

"Amy told me Tige is going to get even with you." She related the rest of Amy's warning about Tige and Lulu, then paused, waiting for his response.

"Don't worry. I'll handle it." Tanner took one step but her hand on his arm stopped him. Her glossy dark brown eyes met his.

"I misjudged you about Amy, didn't I?" she murmured. "She said you went back for her."

"You needed her to say that? You couldn't have trusted that I'm not a total jerk?" Looking at Sophie's beloved face, he felt utterly hopeless. If

God had truly forgiven him for his mistakes, why couldn't He let Sophie love him?

"I'm sorry," she whispered, her voice brimming with regret. But what good was regret?

"It doesn't matter about then," he said, unable to cover the ragged tone of his voice. "It's the past. It has nothing to do with who I am now." He lifted his head, loving her beautiful face, hating that he'd caused her pain. "I'm sorry you won't trust me because I would die for you, Sophie. Because I love you more than life."

Reeling at the pain of never having Sophie's love, Tanner left. He walked to the shed where the fireworks were stored and sank onto an empty crate. There he silently poured out his heart to the only family he'd ever had—his heavenly Father.

"Where are your helpers?" Moses asked, surveying the spotless kitchen Sophie was still scrubbing.

"I sent them home." She glanced at him over one shoulder in concern. "I thought Davy and Beth would be with you."

"They were. Lefty's with them while I grab a coffee." He stepped in front of her. "You cryin', woman?"

"Don't be ridiculous. Why would I be crying?" Sophie sniffed and brushed away the tears from her cheeks. "I've just pulled off the biggest job of my career."

"That make you happy?" Moses asked.

"Ecstatic," she wailed.

"Huh. Funny way of showing it." He surveyed the kitchen, then said in a bland voice, "Hoped maybe you and Tanner finally got things sorted out." Moses poured a cup of coffee and creamed it. "Kid's crazy about you and yours."

"Kid?" she spluttered, ashamed of her tears but unable to stop shedding them.

"Compared to an old man like me Tanner is a kid." Moses grinned as he sat down at the table. "So you don't care about him. Too bad. Never find a better man than Tanner. He's got principles and integrity. Committed to make Burt's dream live. That takes guts."

"I know he's wonderful," she blubbered. Moses ignored her.

"Lots easier on him if he let the dream go. Sure, he'd lose the ranch but he'd still walk away with a big cash settlement and then he could chase his own dreams."

"I don't think Tanner would do that," Sophie said with a frown.

"Glad you at least figured that out about him." Moses shook his head. "'Cause he'd never do it. Not in a million years."

"You sound pretty sure." His certainty irritated her.

"Because I know Tanner." Moses's unblinking stare made her shift uncomfortably.

"You can't say it will never happen," she insisted. "You can't know that."

"'Course I can!" Moses glared at her. "I figured Tanner Johns out a long time ago. If you think he'd break his promise to the man he loved like a father, you're blind! Tanner's one in a million. Ain't nobody else I'd trust with my life more 'n him. Maybe it's a good thing you can't love him."

"Hey!" Sophie protested. "I never said—"

Moses ignored her.

"That boy's got a big job to do getting Burt's camp going." He shuffled to the door. "He sure don't need some 'fraidy-cat lady who won't trust him. You'll just hold him back from doin' the Lord's work."

Tossing her one last glare, Moses stomped out the door.

Indignation filled Sophie at the outspoken old man. But as she refilled the snack trays one phrase kept repeating in her head:

"Some 'fraidy-cat lady who *won't* trust him."

She prided herself on her strength, on her independence. But now she realized that her lack of ability to trust made her weak. Undependable?

*Won't* trust Moses had said.

Was trust merely a matter of will?

"This was a fantastic idea, Tanner." Pastor Jeff stopped him before he could move another box of sparklers into the truck bed. "That group of transient kids you found sleeping in the park the other night are having a ball with Moses. Got some ideas for a program we could start for them?"

"A few." Tanner chatted with the eager pastor for several more minutes, accepting his praise for Sophie's food while wondering if she'd ever come back to Wranglers. She didn't need his jobs anymore. Sophie's cooking had taken Tucson by storm and she was now in high demand.

When Jeff left, Tanner continued loading, praying for God to somehow intervene.

"You're the boss and you still hafta do this menial stuff?"

Tanner whirled around, hating the supercilious note in Tige's voice. He clamped his lips shut on an angry reply when he saw his nemesis had hold of a terrified Davy while Lulu gripped Beth by one arm.

"What are you doing, Tige?" he asked in a careful tone. "Let the kids go. You're scaring them."

"That's the idea, buddy." Evil blazed across his face. "A little insurance policy."

*Lord, help!*

Tanner suppressed his fear and smiled at the children he'd come to love.

"Hey, Beth. Davy. You okay?" They both nodded, obviously waiting for him to do something. "Why do you need insurance, Tige?" he asked, using his best conversational tone, though he already knew the answer because of all the questions Tige had lobbed at him earlier.

Where was security? Lefty? Moses? Sophie? His blood ran cold at the thought of her being trapped by Tige.

"You're a big shot now, Tanner. You're rolling in it with this place." There was a crazy gleam in the gold eyes that said Tige needed a fix and fast. In this state Tanner knew he'd go to extreme lengths to appease his cravings.

"How much do you need?" he asked, hoping he could talk Tige into being reasonable.

"Ten thousand." Triumph shone on Tige's desperate face. "Cash."

"The estate is entailed, buddy." Tanner laughed. "There's no way I could get my hands on that kind of cash," he scoffed. "You think a rich guy like Burt would leave his millions to a street punk like me?"

"He's lying," Lulu hissed.

"I'm not." Tanner tried to visually encourage Davy, who, oddly, seemed to be more nervous than Beth. Then he realized why.

Beth, eyes squeezed closed, was praying. But Tige held to Davy's throat a knife that Tanner recognized as one of Moses's artifacts.

"I got maybe fifty bucks on me," he said, slipping his hand into his pocket. "Nope. Forty," he said as he thumbed through some bills. "Take it." He held it out and almost heaved a sigh of relief when Tige made a forward movement.

"Tanner? Where are you?" Sophie's voice, breathless and oozing worry, preceded her through the bluff of trees that kept them hidden from the rest of the ranch. A moment later she appeared and Tanner's fears multiplied at the eager look on Tige's face.

"Oh, there you are. I can't find—" One look and she immediately assessed the situation. "Are you guys okay?" When she would have stepped forward Tanner grabbed her arm.

"The kids are fine, Sophie." He squeezed her fingers to reassure her. "Tige and I are just talking."

"Yeah." Tige's cackle gave Tanner chills. One slip of that knife against Davy's throat—*Lord, help us.* "We're talking about how much your kids are worth, Sophie. Tanner thinks forty bucks is gonna do it."

"Go back to the house, Sophie," Tanner told her quietly. Her terrified gaze met his. "The kids will be fine, I promise. Go to the house and pray."

"Pray?" Tige and Lulu hooted with derision.

Tanner ignored them. When Sophie didn't move he added, "Trust me. Please? Just this once trust me. I promise I'll protect them with my life."

Knowing he had no clue how to handle this, Tanner watched fear war with trust in Sophie's dark eyes. He ached for the worry he'd caused her. He should never have let her come to Wranglers today, not knowing what Tige was capable of. How many more mistakes did he have to make before he'd give up that silly dream of finally having a family?

"God is our help." Beth's clear voice pierced the tension of the moment.

A rush of joy filled Tanner. What a child!

"Beth trusts God," he said for Sophie's ears alone. "Can you?"

Finally Sophie nodded. "I will trust you both."

Tanner hugged her. *Please don't let me fail her trust.* "Go now," he urged, his lips grazing her ear. "And pray."

Sophie nodded, touched his cheek then turned to Tige. "If you hurt my children," she said through clenched teeth, "you will pay."

With one last look at Beth and Davy, she slipped out the way she'd come.

"Let's settle this," Tanner said with new resolve. "Before Sophie alerts security."

Fear and greed mingled on Tige's face. "I want more than forty dollars, Tanner."

"I've got two hundred tucked away. But I'm not getting it unless you let those children go." Tanner kept his face impassive and unyielding. He held up a closed hand. "I blow this whistle and security will be on you like fleas on a dog. You let the kids go, I'll drop it and we'll get your money." He inclined his head. "Deal?"

As he talked, Tanner kept edging closer to the pair, watching Tige, waiting for his moment. Sophie trusted him. He could not fail her.

"Take it, Tige," Lulu whined. "I'm hurtin'. I need somethin' real bad."

The moment he saw her fingers loosen on Beth, Tanner lunged forward and dragged the little girl free. Seeing what was happening, Davy jerked out of Tige's grip, grabbed Beth's hand and obeyed Tanner's yell to run. Tanner saw Beth and Davy race away and whispered a prayer of praise.

He realized his mistake the moment he felt the knife pierce between his ribs.

"Shouldn't have done that, buddy," Tige said as Tanner folded to the ground. "Now your lady and her kids are gonna pay a lot more than forty bucks." He and Lulu left.

Pain streaked through Tanner's body but he ignored it, knowing Tige would go to the house to hurt Sophie and find that money. Tanner couldn't allow that but in this state he would never be able to beat the couple back there.

"I need help, God." Suddenly he remembered the shortcut through the cacti. It was dark now and it wouldn't be easy to find the trail but it was much shorter. "Help me, Lord."

He pushed his way through, ignoring the thorns scraping his skin as blood seeped through his fingers and ran down his side. It didn't matter. Nothing mattered but proving that Sophie could trust him. Finally he made it to the back door and yanked it open.

"Tanner!" He felt Sophie's hand touch his. He laced his fingers with hers but he kept his focus on the doorway. A moment later Tige and Lulu appeared, dazed and confused.

"How'd he get here so fast?" Lulu asked.

"Here." Tanner held out his forty dollars. "You'll be a wanted man now, Tige. The cops will be here in seconds to arrest you. You'd better take this and go while you can."

Tige glared at him, hate and fear vying for supremacy. He grabbed the cash Tanner held out but before he could race away, Tanner said, "I forgive you, buddy. But don't come back here again unless you want to talk about God."

"Fat chance," Tige said and left with Lulu following.

Woozy now, Tanner grabbed the door frame.

Sophie slipped her arm around his waist, her tearful face inches from his.

"You shouldn't have risked your life, Tanner."

"I had to," he managed to say. "I love you, all of you. You're my world."

He had lots more to add but he couldn't make his mouth say it.

"Don't you dare die on me, Tanner Johns," Sophie said, her voice furious. "Not now. Not after saving my kids. Not before I—"

Tanner wanted so badly to hear this but he couldn't fight the waves of black descending on him.

# Chapter Fourteen

Sophie lowered Tanner's unconscious body to the floor, resisting when Moses tried to pull her back.

"No!" She shoved his hands away and cradled Tanner's head on her lap, praying he wouldn't die before she could tell him how sorry she was that it had taken her so long to finally trust him. "Please God, help Tanner. Please?"

As if in a vacuum, Sophie noticed two security men rush in and heard Davy tell them what had happened. She watched Moses press a white tea towel against Tanner's side, saw it stain a dark crimson red in seconds. She felt Beth curl next to her, repeating verses she'd memorized. But all these things were background. Sophie's focus remained on the man whose lifeless body she held, the man who'd kept his promise.

The man she trusted.

"I can't lose him now, God." Not now that she'd

finally realized that Tanner was a man to trust, to love.

Sophie didn't know how much time passed before Moses insisted she move away so the paramedics could attend to Tanner. She did but watched every move while she answered questions policemen lobbed at her. But when Tanner was loaded on a gurney, Sophie pulled free of Moses's restraining arm to grab Tanner's hand and walk beside him to the waiting ambulance, praying with every ounce of courage she possessed.

"Is the party over?" his beloved voice suddenly demanded.

"For you it is," Moses said in a gruff tone from just behind her. Of course Moses would be there. He loved Tanner, too.

Tanner said nothing for a moment. His eyelids fluttered, then lifted. He glanced around with a frown until he caught sight of Sophie.

"Hello, beloved," he murmured in the most tender voice she'd ever heard.

"Hi." The relief and joy flooding Sophie's heart kept her from saying more.

"Security caught your friends. They're not going to hurt anyone else," Moses said.

"That's good." He licked his lips and blinked again, trying to focus.

"You're going to the hospital now," Sophie explained.

He nodded, obviously groggy. But when he saw the ambulance door open he said, "Wait," in a loud, firm voice.

"Tanner, you need treatment," Sophie insisted. "Don't worry, you won't be alone. I'm going with—"

"No." He squeezed her hand. "Keep the party going. Make sure there are fireworks." He paused, grimaced and exhaled as if the effort to speak was becoming difficult. "I promised the street kids that we would have fireworks in the desert." He managed a crooked smile. "I have to keep my promise to them."

"And you do keep your promises, don't you?" How she loved the way his green eyes crinkled at the corners. "Because that's who you are. I know that now."

"Really?" He waved off the attendant's insistent urging to leave. "Just a minute. It's important."

"Because a stab wound isn't," the woman barked. But she moved back a step.

Sophie looked at Tanner and saw the man he truly was, a man who cherished and protected those he loved. Tanner Johns was the man for her. She knew that now.

"We can talk when I get to the hospital, okay?" Suddenly shy with so many interested onlookers,

Sophie pressed her lips against his in a brief kiss. "I'll see you later, Tanner," she promised.

"Fireworks?" he asked.

"I give you my word that Wranglers Ranch will have the best fireworks for miles around."

"To go with the best eats," he teased in a husky tone.

Sophie couldn't help it. She leaned over and kissed him again.

"Gross." Davy made a gagging sound. "Mom, Tanner's got to get to the hospital. You can do that later." He pulled her arm so she had to back away.

"Thanks, kid." The grateful attendants loaded Tanner but before they could close the doors he called, "Keep praying, Beth."

"I will, Mr. Cowboy," she promised.

Then the doors slammed shut and Sophie lost sight of his smiling face.

Staying put while the ambulance with Tanner left was the hardest thing she'd ever done. And yet Sophie had no fear that Tanner wouldn't be okay. He was in God's hands now. She had no clue how to keep her promise to Tanner but she did know God was going to help her. And He would be with Tanner, too. All she had to do was trust.

"Come on, everyone," she said briskly. "I promised Tanner we'd keep this party going and we're going to do just that. Davy, you find Lefty and bring him here. He should be about finished with his rodeo display by now. Beth, you and I are going to make popcorn to pass around. Moses—"

"I know right well what my job is, missy." His indignation turned to laughter. "You sure grew some courage."

"Tanner taught me. 'If God be for us who can be against us?'" she quoted. "Right, Beth?"

"Yes, Mama." Content that her beloved Tanner was going to be okay, Beth walked inside the house ready to help her favorite cowboy's ranch.

The hands arrived in groups of twos and threes, their faces sober, fear waiting to grab hold. It was up to her to show her faith.

"Tanner's going to be okay," she assured them. "But he wouldn't leave until I promised we'd ensure the fireworks are every bit as great as he promised the kids. To do that, we'll need your help. Can we count on you? Can Tanner?"

"Yes!" they agreed in a cheer. "For Tanner!"

"Great." Teary-eyed at their respect for their boss, Sophie pressed on. She would trust God to help her keep her promise. "Moses says most of our guests don't know about Tanner's stabbing. Let's keep it that way with the celebrations continuing because that's what Tanner wants. Lefty, can you handle the fireworks?"

"I've helped out the city for years. In fact I taught Tanner. No problem." He selected three other men and told her they'd be ready in half an hour.

"Great." She heaved a sigh of relief. *Thank You, Lord, for Lefty.* "Moses, what else do we need?"

"Me and the boys will handle crowd control," the old man said and left immediately with his helpers.

"Davy, you, Beth and I are making popcorn," Sophie said before her son could follow the others.

"Aw, Mom! We didn't mean to get caught by that guy. We were just going to get some carrots for the horses."

"So you disobeyed Lefty and Moses when they told you to stay put."

Their shamed faces were answer enough.

After this evening's events Sophie needed to keep her children close. She'd have to deal with their disobedience later. But for now all she said was, "Do it for Tanner. Okay?" Davy nodded and got to work without complaint.

Somehow everything went off without a hitch. As she watched the spectacular display of lights, Sophie heard *oohs* and *ahhs*, gasps of wonder and squeals of delight with a heart full of thanksgiving. God had helped them fulfill Tanner's goal. As the final starbursts of red, white and blue filled the sky, the crowd burst into the national anthem. When it was over a hushed silence fell. Then Pastor Jeff spoke.

"Before we leave let's pray and thank the God of our land who has blessed us with this place, Wranglers Ranch." Pastor Jeff offered a short prayer, then wished the group a happy Fourth.

Her heart full, Sophie stood in the shadows with an arm around each child and listened to groups of chattering kids as they climbed aboard buses that would return them to the city. There were many positive comments but the best came from a teen who stopped to ask her if he could come back to Wranglers Ranch tomorrow to talk about God.

"Come back whenever you like," Sophie offered. She had no idea what Tanner could do for him but she knew he would do something because Wranglers Ranch was God's ranch and Tanner was committed to doing God's will. She trusted them both.

Now she needed to tell that to Tanner.

Groggy and in pain, Tanner wakened to semi-darkness and Sophie by his bedside, holding his hand. She'd been dozing but must have sensed his return to lucidity for her eyes suddenly opened and she stared straight at him.

"Hello." He stopped, aghast to see tears rolling down her face.

"Thank you for protecting my kids," she sobbed. "But I wish it hadn't cost you so dearly."

Privately Tanner thought a little flesh wound was worth it if meant what he hoped it did. "Sophie—"

"I love you, Tanner," she blurted and dashed the tears from her eyes. "I'm just sorry that you had to get stabbed before I came to my senses and realized that. I also realize God is trustworthy. Even when I didn't feel Him, He was at work for you, for my kids and for me because He loves us with a love I can always count on." A tremulous smile tilted her lovely lips. "Why did it take me so long to trust the gift of love?"

"That's what I'd like to know," he said plaintively. He shifted in the bed so he could gaze at her. That's when he finally realized that in God's eyes his miserable past filled with terrible mistakes didn't matter anymore. God had blessed him with the opportunity to reach kids, and he'd sent Sophie to help.

"Tanner?" Worry tinged the edge of her voice. "Maybe I shouldn't have told you that. Maybe it's too soon—"

"Too soon?" He burst out laughing and then caught his breath as his side reminded him he wasn't totally fit. "I've been in love with you forever, woman."

"Really?" Her big brown eyes gazed at him

with love. "Tell me again, please?" she whispered, squeezing his hand. So he did.

"I love you, Sophie. You make my days bright. I wake up wanting to share ideas with you and go to sleep thinking about all the things we can do together." He saw a tiny smile flutter across her face. "I love the way you challenge me to be better, to do more and to think outside the box. No one has ever cared enough to push me."

"Oh, Tanner." Her eyes clouded.

"Except God," he corrected. "But it took you to help me accept that if I wouldn't let go of the past and accept God's forgiveness, I couldn't do what He needs me to do today." He made a face. "I couldn't 'fan into flame' my so-called 'gift.'"

"It *is* a gift, Tanner." Sophie's eyes pinned him. "Your ability to get people together is a God-given gift. That's what drew me to helping you spread the message of God's love through Wranglers Ra—"

"Sophie," he interrupted.

She looked startled. "Yes."

"My side hurts like crazy. I'm kinda befuddled," he said. "But will you please do something for me?"

"What?"

"Can you please get me a cup of coffee?"

She smiled but shook her head. "Nothing but

water till morning. Sorry." She touched his cheek. "Something else I can do?"

"Oh, yeah." Tanner could hardly believe God had given him this woman to love. "Coffee isn't my top request."

"What is?"

"Will you please kiss me?"

"I was just waiting for you to ask." A pretty flush of color tinted her cheekbones.

"Don't wait anymore, darling Sophie," he pleaded.

She didn't kiss him immediately. Instead her fingers cupped his face, his eyes, traced a path over his nose to his lips and to his chin. Finally she spoke.

"I love you, Tanner. I trust you with my heart." Then Sophie kissed him and when Tanner came back down to earth he decided that kiss and the ones that followed were well worth the wait.

"What are you thinking?" she whispered, her head resting lightly on his heart.

"That for as long as I can remember I've longed for someone of my own, a history, a heritage that I thought would make me worthy of God's love." He smiled. "Instead God sent me to Burt and to you and the kids to teach me that it's not my past that matters, it's what I do with my future."

"Mmm," she agreed.

"You are the love of my life, Sophie. You and

the kids are so precious, Beth with her steadfast joy in life, and Davy with his generosity of spirit." Tanner hesitated, waiting until she lifted her head to look at him. "May I please be part of your family?"

Sophie began to cry. Tanner panicked until she explained.

"I'm crying because I'm so happy," she blubbered.

"I hope I never make you sad, then. I notice you didn't answer my question." He held his breath, exhaling only after she nodded.

"With one caveat."

"Which is?" How he loved her.

"It's *our* family."

"Deal. Seal it." He held out a hand but Sophie made a face.

"Really, Tanner?" She shook her head in reproof. "In this family we'll do things differently." This time she kissed him with a fervor that left Tanner breathless. "Deal?" she asked when she finally drew back.

"Absolutely." He leaned back against his pillow and promptly fell asleep. Deliriously happy, Tanner stirred from his drowsy state only when Sophie called his name. "Yes, love?"

"I forgot to tell you. The fireworks went off without a hitch and your ranch hands have Wranglers back to its pristine state, running smoothly and waiting for your return and the next event you plan."

"Sophie," he protested, cupping her chin in his hand and feathering his finger against her lips. "Do we really have to talk about the ranch right now?"

"Yes." She grinned. "Because Tige's sons asked Lefty if they could stay at Wranglers until they get their lives straightened out. Your retreat to help Tucson's needy kids is happening."

"With God leading, we'll do lots more, my darling Sophie." Tanner kissed the fingers he still held. "When are we getting married?"

The resolution to that issue was soon settled and sealed with a kiss.

# Chapter Fifteen

Sophie married Tanner at a very private ceremony at Wranglers Ranch in September. At least they thought it would be private.

Tanner, having helped with one wedding, confidently assured Sophie he was capable of planning this wedding. He asked Mrs. Baggle to play for the event and insisted Beth choose a fancy dress in her favorite blue. He also bought a suit and Stetson to match his own for Davy and special-ordered cowboy boots for both children. Davy's were black and Beth's where white with blue stitching. Both children walked a little taller in them.

With everything ready, Mrs. Baggle hit a few notes signaling Tanner to walk to the front with his best man, Moses. He was astounded to see the patio filled.

"Who invited all these people?" he whispered to Pastor Jeff.

"Your guests come courtesy of Trent and Rod," Jeff said with a laugh. "You did tell them they were part of the family, remember? They're telling their new friends they intend on staying as long as they can since their parents are locked up. So they told everyone at church about your wedding with some help from Lefty and the other hands."

"Good. The more the merrier." Tanner smiled at Tige's grinning sons.

When Mrs. Baggle played the first chords of "Here Comes the Bride," Tanner inhaled, waiting impatiently to see the woman he so dearly loved. Sophie's neighbor Edna came down the aisle first, without a walker, resplendent in a gown of swirling fall colors, delighted to be part of the event. She took her place beside Moses, favoring him with a sweet smile that was returned so fulsomely that Tanner thought perhaps his friend also had found someone to care about.

Then Sophie appeared. She'd chosen a short ivory lace jacket and matching knee-length skirt that swirled around her pretty knees. Then he saw her boots—ivory, ladylike, lace-up Western boots. He smiled, his delight growing at seeing a jaunty ivory hat perched on the side of her head.

She'd certainly embraced the ranch theme and he loved it, loved her.

Sophie walked slowly toward him, her gaze holding his until she paused just a moment to smile at her kids. Then she moved to stand in front of him.

"Wow!" Tanner barely heard the laughter as he gazed at his beautiful bride.

"Wow yourself," she murmured. "You clean up nice, Mr. Cowboy." Then sliding her hand into his, she turned with him to face Pastor Jeff.

"Friends, we've gathered today to witness the marriage of Tanner and Sophie." He continued to speak, explaining how God had drawn them together. "Sophie and Tanner will now say their vows to each other."

Tanner inhaled. He'd worked so hard to memorize the words that he felt in his heart. He wasn't going to let nervousness mess this up.

"Dearest Sophie. For most of my life I've dreamed of being part of a family, but I never thought I was worthy. Burt offered me unconditional love, but when he died I figured I'd lost my chance to have a family. I sure had no clue how to make his dream come true. Then you came along, sweet Sophie, and hope bloomed. You taught me about love and showed me how to spread it around. From you I've learned to forget the past and focus on God's plan for the future.

Because of you Burt's dream is happening. Because of us." He inhaled, then said the rest unrehearsed, from his heart.

"I promise I'll always be here for you, always love you, and always love Beth and Davy. I promise to work with you, with God leading us, to fan whatever gifts He gives us into flame. I love you, Sophie. And I promise to keep my promises to you. Forever."

He slid the solid gold circle of promise on her finger right next to the diamond solitaire he'd had specially designed just for his Sophie.

"Tanner." Sophie inhaled. A slow smile moved across her face. "I love you. I love the way you cherish me so I feel special. I love the way you encourage and support me. I love your joy in life, your love for my kids, your determination and grit to fulfill Burt's wishes. And I love that you've included me in the Wranglers Ranch ministry. But most of all, I love that I can trust you." She gave him a cheeky grin. "I know it took me a long time to get there but I know now that God knows what He's doing. It's going to be a great life and I can hardly wait to share it with you."

Sophie slid a plain gold band, exactly the style Tanner wanted, on his finger.

Then Tanner kissed the woman whom God had sent him, the one with whom he'd share a wonderful family on the ranch he loved, reaching kids who needed to know about God's love.

In the silence of that precious moment, Beth's voice penetrated.

"Know what, Davy? Mama should have known you can always trust a cowboy."

\* \* \* \* \*

*If you liked this story, pick up these other books from Lois Richer:*

*A DAD FOR HER TWINS*
*RANCHER DADDY*
*GIFT-WRAPPED FAMILY*
*ACCIDENTAL DAD*

*Available now from Love Inspired!*

Dear Reader,

Hi there and welcome to Wranglers Ranch. You're always welcome here. I hope you've enjoyed reading about Tanner's struggle to forgive himself for his past and "fan into flame" the gifts God's blessed him with. Single mom Sophie struggles to trust God again with her kids, her heart and her future, which means she has to let go of the controls and rebuild her faith. Don't we all struggle with trust at some time in our lives?

I hope you'll come back to the ranch this December for Christmas. The kids' camp is really starting to take shape and there are lots of celebrations planned.

Till we meet again I wish you the joy of trusting the One who forgives and forgets, the peace of letting go and letting God, and the blessing of true love that will never end.

I'd love to hear from you via email at loisricher@gmail.com, snail mail at Box 639, Nipawin, Sk. Canada, S0E 1E0 or my webpage at www.loisricher.com.

Blessings,

# LARGER-PRINT BOOKS!

## GET 2 FREE
## LARGER-PRINT NOVELS
## PLUS 2 FREE
## MYSTERY GIFTS

*Love Inspired®*

# SUSPENSE
### RIVETING INSPIRATIONAL ROMANCE

## *Larger-print novels are now available...*

---

**YES!** Please send me 2 FREE LARGER-PRINT Love Inspired® Suspense novels and my 2 FREE mystery gifts (gifts are worth about $10). After receiving them, if I don't wish to receive any more books, I can return the shipping statement marked "cancel." If I don't cancel, I will receive 4 brand-new novels every month and be billed just $5.49 per book in the U.S. or $5.99 per book in Canada. That's a savings of at least 19% off the cover price. It's quite a bargain! Shipping and handling is just 50¢ per book in the U.S. and 75¢ per book in Canada.* I understand that accepting the 2 free books and gifts places me under no obligation to buy anything. I can always return a shipment and cancel at any time. Even if I never buy another book, the two free books and gifts are mine to keep forever.

110/310 IDN GH6P

| | | |
|---|---|---|
| Name | (PLEASE PRINT) | |
| Address | | Apt. # |
| City | State/Prov. | Zip/Postal Code |

Signature (if under 18, a parent or guardian must sign)

### Mail to the **Reader Service:**
**IN U.S.A.:** P.O. Box 1867, Buffalo, NY 14240-1867
**IN CANADA:** P.O. Box 609, Fort Erie, Ontario L2A 5X3

**Are you a current subscriber to Love Inspired® Suspense books
and want to receive the larger-print edition?
Call 1-800-873-8635 or visit www.ReaderService.com.**

\* Terms and prices subject to change without notice. Prices do not include applicable taxes. Sales tax applicable in N.Y. Canadian residents will be charged applicable taxes. Offer not valid in Quebec. This offer is limited to one order per household. Not valid for current subscribers to Love Inspired Suspense larger-print books. All orders subject to credit approval. Credit or debit balances in a customer's account(s) may be offset by any other outstanding balance owed by or to the customer. Please allow 4 to 6 weeks for delivery. Offer available while quantities last.

---

**Your Privacy**—The Reader Service is committed to protecting your privacy. Our Privacy Policy is available online at www.ReaderService.com or upon request from the Reader Service.

We make a portion of our mailing list available to reputable third parties that offer products we believe may interest you. If you prefer that we not exchange your name with third parties, or if you wish to clarify or modify your communication preferences, please visit us at www.ReaderService.com/consumerschoice or write to us at Reader Service Preference Service, P.O. Box 9062, Buffalo, NY 14240-9062. Include your complete name and address.

LISLP15

# REQUEST YOUR FREE BOOKS!
## 2 FREE WHOLESOME ROMANCE NOVELS IN LARGER PRINT
## PLUS 2 FREE MYSTERY GIFTS

✸✸✸✸✸✸✸✸✸✸✸✸✸✸✸✸✸✸✸✸✸✸✸

# HEARTWARMING™

✲✲✲✲✲✲✲✲✲✲✲✲✲✲✲✲✲✲✲✲✲✲✲

*Wholesome, tender romances*

**YES!** Please send me 2 FREE Harlequin® Heartwarming Larger-Print novels and my 2 FREE mystery gifts (gifts worth about $10). After receiving them, if I don't wish to receive any more books, I can return the shipping statement marked "cancel." If I don't cancel, I will receive 4 brand-new larger-print novels every month and be billed just $5.24 per book in the U.S. or $5.99 per book in Canada. That's a savings of at least 19% off the cover price. It's quite a bargain! Shipping and handling is just 50¢ per book in the U.S. and 75¢ per book in Canada.* I understand that accepting the 2 free books and gifts places me under no obligation to buy anything. I can always return a shipment and cancel at any time. Even if I never buy another book, the two free books and gifts are mine to keep forever.

161/361 IDN GHX2

Name _____ (PLEASE PRINT) _____

Address _____ Apt. # _____

City _____ State/Prov. _____ Zip/Postal Code _____

Signature (if under 18, a parent or guardian must sign) _____

### Mail to the **Reader Service:**
**IN U.S.A.:** P.O. Box 1867, Buffalo, NY 14240-1867
**IN CANADA:** P.O. Box 609, Fort Erie, Ontario L2A 5X3

\* Terms and prices subject to change without notice. Prices do not include applicable taxes. Sales tax applicable in N.Y. Canadian residents will be charged applicable taxes. Offer not valid in Quebec. This offer is limited to one order per household. Not valid for current subscribers to Harlequin Heartwarming larger-print books. All orders subject to credit approval. Credit or debit balances in a customer's account(s) may be offset by any other outstanding balance owed by or to the customer. Please allow 4 to 6 weeks for delivery. Offer available while quantities last.

**Your Privacy**—The Reader Service is committed to protecting your privacy. Our Privacy Policy is available online at www.ReaderService.com or upon request from the Reader Service.

We make a portion of our mailing list available to reputable third parties that offer products we believe may interest you. If you prefer that we not exchange your name with third parties, or if you wish to clarify or modify your communication preferences, please visit us at www.ReaderService.com/consumerchoice or write to us at Reader Service Preference Service, P.O. Box 9062, Buffalo, NY 14240-9062. Include your complete name and address.

HW15